PROTECTING NEW YORK

SPECIAL FORCES: OPERATION ALPHA

LAINEY REESE

Dear Readers,

Welcome to the Special Forces: Operation Alpha Fan-Fiction world!

If you are new to this amazing world, in a nutshell the author wrote a story using one or more of my characters in it. Sometimes that character has a major role in the story, and other times they are only mentioned briefly. This is perfectly legal and allowable because they are going through Aces Press to publish the story.

This book is entirely the work of the author who wrote it. While I might have assisted with brainstorming and other ideas about which of my characters to use, I didn't have any part in the process or writing or editing the story.

I'm proud and excited that so many authors loved my characters enough that they wanted to write them into their own story. Thank you for supporting them, and me!

READ ON!
Xoxo
Susan Stoker

DEDICATION

For Carl. I could not have finished this book in time without your kindness, your strength, your love or your support. You are my hero. Thank you for showing me that the love I write about isn't just in my imagination.

Special thanks to Susan Stoker for inviting me in on this project and for letting Dude and Shy come play with me. I love them like they are my own now.

CHAPTER 1

GROUP TEXT BETWEEN CAMI, Ziporah and Evan

C: "Dude? What kind of name is Dude?"

E: "It's his military nickname."

C: "What's his real name?"

E: "Faulkner."

Z: "What the hell kind of name is Faulkner?"

C: "You're one to talk, *Ziporah*. Glass houses and all that."

Z: "Hey! Ziporah is an Old Testament bible name so it's legit, and besides I was named after my Bubbe."

C: "True, true. Still, it's a good thing he's got all those muscles and that hero thing going for him. That's all I'm saying."

EVAN FOUGHT the smile that threatened to break through as he read his wives' playful banter. The two of them were a constant source of joy. And they certainly kept him on his toes.

C: "Muscles? Yes, but the pictures are all bluhky! Evan? Sneak a picture for us? Please???!"

E: "Can't. He's not here yet. Besides. Guys don't take pictures of other guys, Brat."

Z: "Didn't you see him when you looked him up online, C?"

C: "Well, yeah. But the only ones I saw were the grainy newspaper shots from the article when he saved Cheyenne from the bomb."

Z: "Those were the only ones I found too. You could tell he's hot though."

C: "I'd like a cooberating witness."

Z: "Good lord, woman. Put down the phone before you hurt yourself."

EVAN COULD PRACTICALLY HEAR Z's groan. She was an ADA for the city and Cami sometimes threw out random legal jargon to get a rise out of her. It always worked.

Z: "That would be corroborating, moron. And since it's a picture it would be evidence, not a witness."

"WELL, this could go on for days," Evan said under his breath with a smile and tucked his phone into his back pocket. Then he tried to focus on the conversation around him. And not on the raging erection texting with his women always caused.

Before he could pick up the thread, a mountain of a man walked up to their table. Just the sheer force of his presence brought not only the conversation at Evan's table to a standstill, but the tables around them went silent as well. All eyes stayed glued to the newcomer's towering form.

"Faulkner, glad you made it." Brice stood and shook hands with him, then turned to the group. "Gentlemen, I'd like you all to meet Faulkner Cooper. Faulkner, this is my cousin, Cade Marshall, that's Trevor Wellington, the blond Viking is Gage Hollister, then Evan Grant. And you already met my partner, Kent."

Faulkner acknowledged each man in turn with a nod and a handshake, then removed his dark sunglasses as he sat.

"Nice to finally meet you." Evan told him while the waiter filled his water glass. "You've had our boys in blue here all starstruck and dewy eyed ever since they heard you were coming to the police convention."

The others at the table chuckled. Kent plucked a roll from the basket on the table and beaned it at his head. Evan caught it with ease and quirked an eyebrow as he took a huge bite. "Thanks," he said, voice muffled around the mouthful, just to antagonize his friend.

"Is this your first time to New York City, Faulkner?" Cade asked.

"Nah, I've been here a couple times before, but it's my wife's first time. She's bouncing-off-the-walls excited."

Evan was struck by how talking about his wife transformed the man's entire demeanor. It went from intimidating and a little scary to approachable and soft.

"That's great," Cade told him. "There is a never-ending list of things she will want to see and do while you are busy with the conference."

Faulkner nodded hesitated a bit at that. "Yeah. She has a bunch of shit she'd like to see, but she's a small-town girl. She'd probably never admit it, but I think your big city has her cowed. She told me she's gonna chill at the hotel until I get done so we can do her sightseeing in the evenings together."

"Oh, you look thrilled at that plan," Brice said with a laugh.

"Hey, I got an idea," Trevor chimed in. "Both Riley and Terryn have the next three days off—why don't we hook the ladies up and they can show her around? Save you the horrors of tour buses and museums. Besides, a lot of the touristy stuff closes shop pretty early—this way she won't miss out on anything."

"That'd be great," Faulkner said with a genuine smile. "You sure your ladies won't mind spending their off time playing tour guide?"

"Nah," Trevor piped in. "Riley loves this city. She still sees it with the eyes of a tourist herself. She's gonna flip when we give her somebody new to show it off to."

He wasn't the only one who called out with an "I hear that" or something similar. Evan and his friends were a tight-knit group and Riley's love of New York was well known and shared by all. They all loved the city and her enthusiasm for it was truly infectious.

"That's great, then. I'll give Shy a call. She's gonna love having her own personal tour guides."

"Shy?" Gage asked.

"Cheyenne," Faulkner answered. "Shy for short."

"You gentlemen ready to order?"

While the waitress took their orders, Evan

watched Faulkner as he interacted with both the waitstaff and his friends.

The man had an intensity to him that was compelling, to say the least. There was a quality that fit right in with the rest of his dining companions. All but Detective Kent were Sexual Dominants in committed BDSM relationships with their wives. And the striking man sitting across from him was cut from the same cloth. If Evan were a betting man, he'd lay money on Faulkner having some decidedly Master-like behaviors in the bedroom.

"Brice has been excited as a schoolgirl about you coming to the conference and giving your lecture as the preeminent explosives expert," Trevor was saying. "But what he didn't tell us was which branch of the military you're from."

"I'm a SEAL."

Then, like a typical stoic Dom, he left it at that. No elaboration or further comment.

Evan was confident he wasn't the only one who picked up these clues. The men at this table were among the finest Doms he'd ever met, each at the Master status. Not much got by any of them. He felt a smile tug at the corner of his mouth as the evening he had envisioned—polite and proper dinner party with polite and proper conversation—was replaced with new and exciting possibilities.

It was a crying shame that he and his wives were not able to make it tonight. The Coopers were here for an additional three nights, however, and he was going to make it a point to not miss out on the next night's festivities.

CHAPTER 2

TWO HOURS LATER, FAULKNER "DUDE" Cooper let himself into his hotel suite. What was supposed to have been a one-hour obligation lunch with a couple of the detectives in charge of the convention had stretched into two-plus hours of interesting conversation with compelling and dynamic men. He had been pleasantly surprised and was now looking forward to his daytime hours as well as the nighttime ones he would spend with the love of his life.

"You're back."

Speaking of which...

Cheyenne emerged just then from the bathroom. God, he loved his woman. There she stood, dressed in a white fluffy towel with another wrapped turban-style around her dark hair. Shy wasn't too tall and she wasn't too short. She was slender without being bony and had just the right amount of softness to her to make a man never want to leave a bed as long as she was in it.

"I didn't expect you back until after six. I would have started getting ready sooner otherwise." Cheyenne held her towel up between her breasts with one hand while she self-consciously patted at the one wrapped around her head and chewed at her bottom lip.

"For what I have in mind," he said as he stepped toward her, "you're plenty ready."

"Oh, no you don't." She flushed and it literally made his mouth water to see her still-damp skin turn a warm rose. "I know that look. And as fun as that sounds, aren't you going to get in trouble or something?" She started backing up, a smile that she couldn't quite prevent tugging at the corners of her lips.

The need to have her and have her now was too strong to be denied.

"The important stuff they needed me for was all taken care of before lunch. I can skip out on the rest of today's crap. It ain't gonna be near as fun as this." Then, before she could respond, he snatched the towel from her body and flung it over his shoulder. Her squeal was music to his ears, her naked body a decadent feast for his eyes.

"Dude!" she exclaimed as her hands first flailed for a bit, then covered her juicy breasts. "I don't have any makeup on yet. And I bought some pretty lacy things to wear for you too."

"I like what you're wearing just fine." His eyes lifted from her delectable body to her lock with hers. "Shy. Hands down at your sides."

She loved when he got bossy with her during sex as much as he did, and the deepening of her blush proved it.

"But," she wailed even as she complied, "my hair is in a towel. I look ridiculous."

"I think you look adorable," he told her and decided to rattle her a little by taking a slow walk around her. She stayed put, as he knew she would. Shy was his equal in every way and she loved his dominant streak as much as he loved her submissive one.

"You'd think I looked adorable if I was dressed in burlap and covered in hives," she told him with a snort.

"Your point?" he asked with one brow cocked.

"Well—" she started to reply, but Dude reached out to trail his left hand along her collarbone in a firm, smooth glide, and the words died on her still-parted lips.

There was a time in his life when he would have

hesitated before using his ruined left hand, with its missing fingers and mangled scars. Shy had never once cringed from his scars, however, and had in fact told him repeatedly that in her eyes, they made him even sexier. To her, they were proof of his heroism and his service to their country. So now he saw nothing but deepening desire in her expression as he ran that hand over her dewy flesh to cup one trembling breast.

"You're beautiful, Shy," he told her in a voice gone deep with desire. "So fucking beautiful."

Whatever she'd opened her mouth to reply was lost when he closed the distance between them and sealed his lips to hers.

Her kiss was as lush as her figure and the way her tongue slipped in to tangle with his caused something almost savage to come to life inside him. His Shy always had this effect on him—if anything, it only got stronger with time.

Dude cupped the back of her neck to hold her still as he deepened the kiss. He angled her head for a better fit and when her turban shifted, he tugged it off and away. Her dark hair fell in wet ropes around her pretty face, a couple even landing on his nose and cheek, surrounding him in the delicious scent of her shampoo.

"Mmm," he murmured as he pulled back. "You

smell"—he came back to lick at her puffy lips—"and taste delicious." She always wore flavored lip gloss and she knew how much it pleased him. "You already put on lip gloss?" he asked with a smile as he continued to nibble at the lips in question.

"Yeah, salted caramel." Her answer was breathy. Her voice had dropped a couple octaves with her desire, he was happy to note. "Moisturize before you dry off. That's the rule. Body and face. That includes the lips."

A low needy sound emerged from him while he dipped his head. He took a nip at a particularly sensitive spot on her shoulder and let his hands wander where they would, filling themselves with the glory that was his woman.

"Is that your magic secret?" he asked while the silky feel and intoxicating scent of her fired his need to dangerous levels. "Is that how come I can't keep my hands and mouth off of you?"

If she answered, he didn't hear it over the need churning in his gut. Given the size of the suite and the fact that they'd barely made it past the bathroom door, the bed was too far away. Instead, with a growl, he clamped his hands on the succulent globes of her ass and lifted her until her legs wrapped around his hips.

His Cheyenne was no passive lover. Submissive,

yes, but not passive. She clamped on to him with a hunger that matched his in every way. He could feel the heat of her sweet core pressed against his cock as she used every bit of strength she had to grind against him.

He was lucky to make it to the couch. When he did, he fell back on it with a grateful groan and adjusted them both until he had one foot braced on the floor for leverage, Shy on top of him.

"Oh fuck yeah," he exclaimed when she sat back and he got a look at her naked body perched atop his still fully clothed one. "Shy. Reach between us and open my pants. Then take me out, baby. Hurry."

Her hands fumbled as she did as she was told. They faltered even more so when he lifted his head and latched on to one of her tightly budded nipples.

As soon as he was freed, she maneuvered until he was poised to enter her.

"Stop," he ordered, though it made his teeth clench to wait even a second longer. "Hands behind your back. That's it. Now keep them there and don't move."

Careful not to dislodge himself, he lifted until he could wrap his arms around her, then clamped a hand on each of her wrists. He kept her arms folded behind her. The complete trust she placed in him never failed to fire his blood, and today was no exception. As he tightened his grip and adjusted his hold until their torsos were perfectly aligned, all in his world was perfect.

"Brace yourself, Shy," he warned. "And I want you to stay as still as possible for me. Okay?"

When she only nodded, her ragged breath an indication that he wasn't the only one ready to burst, he kissed her tasty lips hard and quick. "Words, Shy. You know I need to hear your words."

"Okay." Breathy, trembling and sexy as hell. "Okay. I'll be still."

And that was all he needed. In one fluid movement, he laid their upper bodies back to the couch, still keeping her arms manacled behind her, and slid inside with one sharp plunge.

His cock swelled even more as the heat of her saturated him. That heat ignited a fire in his soul, a hunger that would never be satiated and a thirst that would never be quenched. Dude's mind was a kaleidoscope of images, swirling and incandescent. Her lovely bouncing breasts, her passion-ravaged face, the root of his shaft wet and glistening as he withdrew, then the sight of her sex-swollen lips when they welcomed him back in. It was a miracle his fucking mind didn't snap from the pleasure of it.

She was poised above him, her beautiful face marked with desire as his hips beat out a fast and furious tempo into hers. Holding her like this, Dude was able to use Shy's weight to pull her into his thrusts so the position put friction on her clit. Neither of them were going to last. She was tight and wet and felt like God himself had designed her to fit only him.

Just when he thought he was going to have to stop so he wouldn't come before she did, he felt it. Shy's body tightened around his and her cries turned to wails. Dude brought her in closer still and let his hips fly, pounding up into her wet and pulsating heat so the climax would come in like a hurricane.

She gave herself up to it and him completely. Dude thought his heart would fly right out of his chest when she pressed her forehead to his and locked eyes with him. When she did this, let him see what his lovemaking did to her, it demolished his self-control. With a howl he didn't bother to bite back, Dude let go and followed her over that cliff.

And as they both panted and shuddered in the throes of it, they never broke that scintillating eye contact.

LATER, as they lay tangled together, listening to their heartbeats return to normal, Dude spoke. "Shy? I wanna talk to you about something. I know you are new to the kinkier side of sex, and baby I can't tell you what it means to me that you have put your trust in me so far."

He felt her smile where her cheek rested on his chest.

"I love what you do to me. Everything you do to me." Her hesitant whisper was like a shot of whiskey, filling his gut with warmth and his head with all sorts of ideas.

"I was hoping we could take our time together here to turn things up a notch or two."

"What do you mean?" she asked, lifting up a little to look him in the eye.

"Well, the guys I was talking to at lunch today are Doms. Like me." She jolted. "Well, not exactly. They are into a lot of stuff that I haven't felt the need to explore. Yet." He cupped her beloved face and stroked his thumb over one silken cheek. "I'd like to explore some of those things here. It'll be new for you. I've been to clubs before, but you haven't. So, we won't take this step until you are a hundred percent ready for it. I mean it, Shy. Don't just say yes because you wanna please me. That'll just piss me off. I want you to think about it and only say yes if you are completely sold on the idea."

"Well," she told him, and he could see her taking him seriously and actually thinking it through.

"What exactly are we talking here? You told me you weren't into whips and chains and that the clubs weren't your scene. Has that changed?"

"No," he started, smiling at the memory. "I haven't changed my mind. See, for a lot of the people in the club scene, it's about protocol. Calling me Sir and shit like that. Most of the subs have to kneel and can't make eye contact. A lot of—I don't know... To me it looks like play acting and dress up. So, yeah. I'm still not into *that.* Or into anything that would cause you pain. Tonight, however, we're going to skirt that stuff and explore the parts of it that I *am* into."

She nodded. "Okay. That makes sense. Wait. You're not talking like, wife swap or orgies are you?" Her face fell and she blurted, "You're not going to try to make me watch you with another woman, are you?"

"Oh God, no!" His own horror matched hers. "No, Shy. Never. You know you're it for me. And God help the poor bastard who tries to lay a hand on you."

Her relief was so evident she simply melted over him with it.

"Thank the lord," she told him. "You had me scared for a minute there." Then she knocked the wind right out of him when she added, "As long as that's straightened out, you know you can do anything to me that you want. You know I trust you. And I've loved everything so far so, yeah. Bring it."

"I'm one damn lucky bastard, you know that?" He kissed the crown of her head and she squeezed him back in response. "So, full disclosure. If we go along for the full night's plans, it'll mean sex in front of other people. And them having sex in front of us too. No touching, obviously, and not like all mashed together. We'll have our own station to play in, but people will be watching."

She was still as she mulled that over. "Are you okay with that, Faulkner? Having other men see me naked? Watching you take me?"

"I'm glad you asked, honey." He rubbed her back and lower until he had a handful of her juicy ass. "If it were in a different setting? Hell no. Not at all. But in a club that's designated specifically for BDSM? Yeah. Because in there, it's like another world. The people who are in the scene don't look at sex and nudity the same way as the rest of the world. For them, it's about embracing our natures and who we are. It's about having a safe place to explore your desires, free of limits and free of judgments."

He felt her nod as she took that in.

"I can see that," she said, surprising him. "What? I'm in love with a Dom. You think I didn't hit the

Internet and do some research? I had to know what I was getting myself into."

When he chuckled and shook his head, the grin she shot him was pure mischief.

"Like I said. As long as you and me are only going to touch and be touched by you and me, I'm good."

A look that had his cock twitching came over her face and she clasped her hands behind his neck. Slowly, so he felt the press and drag of her breasts over his chest and the columns of her supple thighs as they slid over his, she pulled herself up his body so she could whisper in his ear, "I'm very curious about flogging. Just so you know."

Then she slipped out of his arms and out of reach. As she walked away, she taunted him using her most sultry voice. "Your mouth is open, honey."

CHAPTER 3

No one paid any attention to the slim young man in the blue coveralls. He looked innocuous and commonplace as he made his way through the busy building toward the warren of staff-only hallways leading to the boiler room. He kept his head down and talked to no one, even pretended to not understand English when a woman stopped and asked for directions to the bathrooms.

It was crucial to his plan—to their plan—that he go undetected as long as possible. Miguel Delgado was only seventeen years old and on the small side. His mother had drilled into him how important it was to use those things to his advantage during this crucial step in their mission.

"You must not get caught, Miguelito." His mother's face, wan and ravaged from hate-fueled grief,

implored him even in her absence. *"You disguise your-self as a worker, and get to the heart of that building. Act like you belong there and everyone will believe that you do."*

"I still think I should just look like a kid the whole time, Ma. Nobody pays attention to kids."

He should know. Not even she had noticed him really, until both his older brothers had been taken away from her. Invisibility had become his super-power. At only five-three and barely over a hundred pounds, he could still get into movies at kid's prices. He slipped easily through crowds and had become an adept pickpocket. Because even when people notice their missing wallets, the sweet-faced, clean-cut kid in scuffed jeans and a baseball cap was the last person anyone would suspect.

His ability to pass himself off as a ten-year-old had helped him get away with everything, all the way up to grand theft auto. All he had to do was remember to not panic if shit got real and someone caught on. *Just be a kid,* he'd remind himself. More than once, he'd ditched a car and jumped on a swing in a playground while the stupid cops whizzed right past him.

This time, he was banking on his looks to help him get away with murder.

He had to get past this part first. Ma had warned

him this was going to be the hardest. He couldn't grow a beard or even develop a five o'clock shadow, so he'd stolen one from a costume store. It looked fake as hell to him, but his mother had told him as long as he kept his head down and walked like he belonged there and knew where he was going, no one would notice.

So far, she'd been right. He had a wig too, also stolen. Miguel liked his hair close cut so he didn't have to bother with washing or combing it, but he and his mother had agreed that people would remember him more clearly if he was well groomed. Instead, the wig was black and shaggy. Not overly long for a man, but it framed his face and helped conceal the shape of his features.

At least, that was what Ma had told him. She was smart. Smarter than the reporters back home had given her credit for when they'd come to interview her about his brothers.

Carlos, the oldest, had been the first to die. Shot down in cold blood by the police as he and his friends had tried to escape. Sure, they'd rigged a bomb to some stupid girl and were using her as their shield, but what else were they supposed to do? How else could they have gotten away? The cops had had them surrounded and trapped in that fucking store.

If things had gone as planned, Carlos and his buddies would've just robbed the place, taken what they wanted and gone on their way. Nobody had to get hurt. The cops were supposed to protect and serve. Everybody. Not just the people who paid their taxes and shit, but all people. Instead, they'd shot his brother down like a dog and Miguel's life hadn't been the same since.

The grief and outrage had been felt by more than just him. Even the media had understood and they'd done all these interviews with his family and the families of the other guys who had been killed too. At first, the news had told the truth. They had done exposés on police brutality and racism—even though Carlos had been the only non-white guy in his gang, Miguel guessed he would've probably been spared if he'd been white, seeing as how he was the leader.

At least, that was what Ma said.

The whole city had been behind them at first, and there had been candlelight vigils and flowers from all over the state. People knew justice hadn't been served that day and for once, they weren't keeping quiet. The problem was, other than bitching in the news, nobody was *doing* anything about it. The cops who pulled the trigger never even got investigated as the shooting was termed *justified* and the slut who had gotten them shot got away scot-free. That asshole SEAL had saved her and disarmed the bomb, so Carlos's last act before he'd been gunned down had been stolen from him.

Javier, his other brother, had been pissed. Pissed off at the cops and the stupid slut and her SEAL. He had gone to every vigil and rally to try and make a difference, try to make somebody *do* something to make those responsible pay for the lives they'd taken. But nobody had listened. Not to him and not to the others who protested with him.

Only one person had understood his family's rage, shared it with them. Alicia had also lost a brother that day, and from the first time she and Javier met at one of the rallies, they had fallen hard for each other.

When the media got tired of their story and let it fade away, Javier and Alicia hatched a plan and took matters into their own hands. They set out to get the revenge their brothers deserved. They had almost gotten away with it too.

Kidnapping the same stupid bitch and a couple of her friends thrown in for distraction had been a brilliant plan. Until it had backfired.

Now Miguel's mother had lost two sons. Javier

was still alive, but he was in jail and might as well be dead too. Twenty to life, they'd given him. Twenty to life for what? Nobody had even died that time. Sure, if their plan had worked, every single person in that apartment building would have died in the blast, not in vain. Their sacrifice would have been the starting point of a whole new era of change. A testament to the lives that had been lost to police brutality and cover-ups.

As far as Miguel's Ma was concerned, they should have given him a medal, not a life behind bars.

Miguel's anger simmered low and hot in his gut as he pulled out the employee key card he'd lifted from one of the maintenance men. He hoped the guy hadn't reported it lost yet. If it had been, he'd just steal a new one but that would be a delay. And his Ma had told him, delays only led to mistakes.

Get in and get the fuck out.

When the little light flashed green and he heard the lock click, Miguel felt vindicated, as though getting in so easy was a sign that he was on the right path. He was careful to shut the door behind him when he entered the hall, then pulled his phone from his pocket. He shot a quick text home.

Im in.

See? I told you. Its your brother looking out for you from above.

As he slid the phone back into his pocket, he made his way down the halls. Ma had made him memorize the blueprints of this building until he saw them in his sleep. He could've made his way there blindfolded without missing a turn.

When his Ma had seen in the papers that the SEAL and his slut were going to New York City so he could be hailed as a hero, she had been so pissed she'd screamed until her voice broke. The guy was here to teach, for fuck's sake—teach cops how to deactivate bombs and kill innocent people. Ma knew then that it was time. Time to send Miguel, her youngest, out to seek revenge for them all.

And in this city, on a scale as big as this? The whole world would be watching and they'd see. Miguel was going to make them all see what happened when you messed with the Delgados.

"Do you think my hair looks all right?" Cheyenne asked as she fussed in the mirror. Since Riley and Terryn were taking her sightseeing tomorrow, they had thought it would be a good idea if everybody got together for dinner tonight as a sort of ice breaker. Before the kinky festivities began.

She'd come a long way from the slightly insecure woman she'd been before Dude had come into her life. Having the love of a man so handsome and compelling did wonders for self-esteem. Wherever they went together, heads would turn, male and female. It gave her confidence a real boost, because she never felt they were mismatched. In every way, he treated her as an equal and the people who saw them together did too. She never got the feeling that people were wondering what a hot hunk of man was doing with her, so after a while, she'd quit wondering too.

But the real game-changer for Shy had been the love of his friends.

Shy had tried her whole life to figure out why her own mother and sister had never loved her. Until she'd met Faulkner and the people who came with him, she'd internalized the pain and rejection, accepting the fault must somehow lie within her.

Faulkner's SEAL team was as tight as brothers and the women they loved, sisters. In one fell swoop, Cheyenne had gone from isolated loner to part of a loud, close-knit family. The women had embraced her from the very first night and she loved them as fiercely as if they were sisters in truth. And being a part of that, a member of a family that loved uncon-ditionally, had abolished a lifetime of self-doubts.

Once in a while, though, old habits would creep up. When Faulkner had told her about the women's offer, she'd had to fight back her first response—to decline and go alone—and instead opened herself up to the possibility of new friends and seeing the city from the eyes of locals.

"It looks beautiful." Dude wrapped his arms around her from behind, placing a sweet kiss on the back of her neck, which sent chills racing down her spine. "Everything about you is beautiful to me. Always." She saw him lean back so he could take a more thorough look, then he added, "I like all those fat curls. How do you get them to stay put like that?" When he lifted a hand to try and find the answer for himself, Shy ducked under his arm and away before he could touch.

"It's a girl secret." She teased him with her hands lifted to ward him off. "If I told you, they'd kick me out of the club and make me give my vagina back."

That surprised a full-bellied laugh out of him that lasted long enough for her to make her getaway to the suite's living room. When he followed, she made sure to keep the coffee table between them in case he got it in his head to try again.

"Seriously," she said with echoes of her own laughter still in her voice. "It may look like I just threw it up last second because I didn't want to bother. But you were here the whole time. I know you heard me cursing and grumbling the entire hour it took me to get it to look like this." With hands on her hips, she glared at him. "Don't even think of touching it and ruining all my hard work."

A challenge of any kind wasn't easy for her man to turn away from, but when she threw down a gauntlet, Faulkner never failed to rise to the occasion. However, he also knew she was nervous about this evening so she was almost sure he wouldn't touch. Almost.

To up her odds, she diverted his attention. "What about the dress? You think this is okay for tonight? Not too much black? Should I add a scarf or some jewelry?"

The dress was new. It was a cool brisk night so she'd chosen a sweater dress, solid black and long sleeved. It was saved from being too severe by the deep vee in both the front and back, showcasing her average cleavage and magically transforming it to well above average.

She loved the skirt too—it flared with her steps and was so responsive she hadn't been able to resist a girl-like swirl when she'd first put it on. Paired with some killer red pumps and she felt like a million bucks.

Cheyenne felt a flush of pleasure when Faulkner

took his sweet time to look her over thoroughly. "Don't change a single fucking thing."

"Thanks." She lowered her eyes and rocked back on her heels a bit. "You look pretty damn hot yourself, there."

Boy, did he ever. Dressed in designer jeans and a gray silk dress shirt, he looked good enough to eat.

"You keep looking at me like that, Shy," he said in his deep sexy as hell voice, "and we're not leaving this room."

She opened her mouth to tell him that actually sounded like a plan she could work with but the shrill ring of the hotel room phone broke the sexual tension like a splash of icy water, so she answered it instead.

"Hello?" Shy tried not to giggle as Faulkner glowered and crossed his arms over his massive chest. "Oh, thank you. Tell them we'll be right down."

Their hotel was home to one of the finest and most sought-after chefs in New York City. It had come as a pleasant surprise, and she and Faulkner had agreed readily when the others asked if they wouldn't mind eating in the hotel's restaurant tonight.

"Too late to back out now." What felt like a thousand frogs doing the Irish step dance in her belly brought an anxious sweat to her palms and a tingle to the back of her neck. "Or is it?" she added, only half joking.

Faulkner shook his head in mock disappointment and even pursed his lips. "What would Alabama and Summer say if they could see you now? Tryin' to chicken out."

He tsked at her for emphasis and it worked. The steel came back to her spine at the mention of some of the other girls among their friends. Cheyenne's momentary nerves disappeared as fast as they'd come.

"Just kidding. Kinda," she added, because who was trying to fool? Dude saw through her to the bone. When it came to the woman he loved, he didn't miss even the smallest detail.

One of the many reasons she loved him back.

Shy walked into the dining room on Faulkner's left, clinging to his scarred and damaged hand like it was her lifeline. Because it was. His hand served as a daily reminder to her. If he could face what he had done to earn those scars and live to tell the tale, then anything she had to face would be a cakewalk in comparison.

"Good evening, sir, ma'am," the hostess greeted them as they approached her glossy podium. "Do you have a reservation for tonight?"

"Yes, we're meeting some friends. I see them over

there; we'll seat ourselves," Faulkner told her politely, barely stopping as he made his way. Shy took a deep breath and told herself to relax.

Then she got a look at the table they were headed toward and almost chickened out.

These people all looked like movie stars. The men as well as the women. She reminded herself that they were just people; no more special than her or anybody else. No matter if they all looked like they could buy and sell entire cities and spent their days sipping mimosas on yachts.

"Hi." One of the women popped up from her seat with a beaming smile and wrapped Shy in a hug before she knew that was her intent.

Cheyenne felt more at ease instantly.

"I'm Riley. I'm a hugger, so if you're not"—she pulled back to grin at Shy and there was an irresistible twinkle in her eyes—"sorry 'bout that."

"No." Cheyenne was quick to reply with a matching grin. "Hugging is good. I'm all for a good hug to break the ice."

And it was true. As simple a gesture as it was, it had worked. Shy was more comfortable now.

"Yay." Riley slipped one hand around Shy's waist, then pointed out each person in turn as she made the introductions. When she finished, she gave

Cheyenne another heartwarming hug and took her seat between her two husbands.

Wow. Two. Hat's off to the spunky little brunette. Cheyenne had her hands full with just one man; and she didn't think she had it in her to take on two.

Shy cut her eyes toward her husband. He was compelling and handsome and his time in the military had honed him into a fierce and steadfast man that she had—from the very first—trusted implicitly. Thank God there weren't two of him. She'd never be able to keep up.

"I'm so excited for tomorrow." Terryn, the stunning redhead on her right, gushed, then reached out and gave Shy a friendly hand squeeze as soon as she was seated. "Riley and I have been brainstorming all our favorite places. Tell us, are you a shopping kind of girl or a monument type?"

"This is important information," Riley added with a look so solemn you'd think she was talking about world peace. "Your answer will determine which routes we take."

Shy laughed a little and gave a shrug.

"If shopping is your thing, then we are going to spend a lot of time in the biggies, you know? Saks, Bloomies, Soho and the Fashion District. But if shopping is not high on your priority list, then we can do stuff like the Statue of Liberty and the Empire State. And Times Square, of course. But that is always better at night."

"Little one." Trevor snagged one of Riley's hands and brought it to his lips. "Let the woman have a chance to order before you start in." He kissed her trapped fingers, then brought their clasped hands to his lap before turning to talk to Shy.

"You're in for a treat. Her questions actually have a legitimate purpose. Nobody loves this city like our girl here and she will tailor your route tomorrow to fit exactly to your interests." The affectionate pride he felt was plain on his face and Shy found it charming as hell.

"That's good to know actually," she told him with a smile. "Thanks. As for shopping, I'm a girl. I like shopping, but I really want to see everything. Can we fit in shopping and the other stuff or will that be too much? I don't want to be a bother or take up too much of anyone's time."

"Oh, don't give that a second thought," Brice, the detective who looked like Superman without the tights, told her. "These two have not been off the phone since we told them about you. It's like Christmas came early."

"You know it," Terryn said.

"You got that right," Riley said at the same time.

"Okay, got it." Cheyenne laughed and held up her water glass in a salute. "I will quit second guessing my good fortune and just wallow in it instead."

The girls lifted their own glasses and gave hearty "hear hears" and Shy felt the rest of her lingering apprehension melt away.

Pleasantries were exchanged—questions like, "Do you have kids?"

To which she answered, "Yes, one girl, Taylor. She's staying with our close friends, Tex and Melody, while we're away. How about any of you?"

Both women were mothers as well. Riley had two —one with each of her men—and they were trying for a third while Terryn and Brice just had one daughter so far.

"And she's such a little hellion, I don't know that either of us have the energy for another," Brice told them with an affectionate laugh.

This was a topic Shy had no trouble discussing and as she and the others launched into stories of births and toddler antics the whole wonder of the evening just hit her.

There she was, West Coast small-town girl at a table in a world-renowned hotel having dinner with *GQ* men and runway-model women in freaking New York City. It was like a crazy dream and seriously already one of the best nights of her life.

Then her phone buzzed, alerting her to an incoming text.

"Yikes." She grimaced as she fished it out of her purse. "I'm so sorry about this, guys. I have it off for everybody except Melody and Tex, so this must be about our daughter."

To a chorus of "no problem" and "of course", Shy unlocked her cell and read the headline.

She was confused because it said it was a text from Dude. She gave him a quizzical look as she tapped to open the message. He didn't make eye contact, which was odd because somehow she knew he could tell she was trying to catch his attention.

It didn't take her long to understand why he wouldn't look her way.

Shy. I told you we were stepping things up tonight.

It starts now.

I've programmed my phone so that throughout the evening you will be getting instructions from me. You are to follow each to the letter, without comment or hesitation.

Shy gasped and looked again toward Dude.

"Is something wrong?" Terryn asked, obviously concerned.

She saw Faulkner bite back a grin even as he lifted his glass to hide the effort. The cad.

"Um." She met Terryn's gaze and tried to appear

cool and calm as she answered, "Everything is fine. It's not bad news."

Cheyenne was pretty sure her face was fire-engine red and there was smoke coming out of her ears as she looked back to her phone.

I want you to excuse yourself from the table. Go to the restroom, take off your panties and bring them back to me.

Cue a giant gasp that she quickly disguised as a cough.

"Hey, I'm—" Cheyenne only fumbled a little as she took her purse off the back of her chair, draped it over her shoulder and stood. "It's nothing serious. But will you please excuse me? I just have to—um—go to the restroom for a moment."

"Oh! Potty break," squealed Riley as she threw her napkin on the table and hopped to her feet. "Mwa!" She planted a kiss first on Trevor's cheek, then Cade's. "Be right back."

"Thank God." Terryn's napkin surrendered to the table too as she stood. She ran a hand over Brice's shoulder as she rounded past him. "I thought I was gonna bust waiting for one of you to say you had to go too."

"You could have said you needed to go to the bathroom?" Exasperated, Riley gave the slender redhead a hip bump. "I totally would have come with."

They all started on their way, and Cheyenne tried to appear as though she were listening to the conversation instead of what she was really listening to: the panicked squeal-ly voice in her head saying over and over *"Omg Omg Omg Omg Omg Omg Omg Omg!"*

"No, I know. I just didn't want to be the one to break the moment. You know?" Terryn was saying, gesturing and looking toward both Shy and Riley. "Wasn't it going really great in there? Like, the conversation was almost like one of the movie montages of what a dinner party is supposed to be. Don't you think?"

"You're right! It was so fun. I get why you didn't want to interrupt. The energy around the table *was* really great." Riley looked at Shy and asked, "Did you feel it too? I hope you weren't uncomfortable this whole time. That would be awful." Her lovely face blanched a little at that.

"No." Shy laughed, reached out and gave her a little one-armed hug before they fell back into step together. "God, no. I was having a great time. In fact, just before my phone buzzed I'd been thinking this had to be one of the best nights of my life."

They had reached the bathrooms and now stood

in the beautifully decorated sitting room adjacent to the stalls.

At the mention of her phone, Shy tensed, hoping she hadn't sparked an interest in the message that had sent her here in the first place. She'd never know how to explain it.

"So what are you supposed to do in here?"

CHAPTER 4

SHY FROZE and stared at Riley's cheerfully inquisitive face like a deer fixated on headlights.

"Huh?" *Oh, clever, Cheyenne. Real witty.*

"You got instructions from your Dom. Right?" Terryn prompted, like she was telling Shy her bank had called.

No biggie. Happens every day.

"Is it something difficult? Do you need help? Or privacy? We could block the door for you—?"

She looked over her shoulder toward the door in question and Cheyenne felt her mouth drop open when Riley chirped, "Ooh! Good idea." And ran to do just that.

"Wait," Shy called out, flabbergasted. "What?" She looked from one beautiful smiling face to the next and felt a million questions bubbling up.

She was a bit surprised at the one that made it out first.

"Are you two in on this?"

Shocked laughter was her answer.

"Of course not," Riley said. "But, we're both subs too and we know a Dom maneuver when we see one. Right, T?" She nudged her friend with her elbow.

"Right," Terryn answered with a wink toward Shy. "And we know the signs of a happy yet flustered sub."

"Oh my God." Cheyenne couldn't find words. She'd known coming in that these girls were sexual submissives to their Doms. What she hadn't realized was what that would mean for her.

Friends in the same position she was in. Friends who could offer advice and, more importantly, confidantes who shared the same experiences she did.

Her circle of friends back home were more than sisters to her, and she knew she could talk to them about anything. And they would be open, supportive, and never judgmental. But they also couldn't tell her what it felt like to be flogged. Or which kind of lubricant was the best for anal plugs.

These women could.

"Holy shit, guys," she blurted. "I forgot you two

knew about this stuff. Oh, thank you little fat baby Jesus." They all chuckled as Shy flopped into a chair and rubbed a hand on her belly. "My stomach about dropped to my feet for a minute there. I didn't know how I was going to tell you beautiful sweet girls that I had to go take off my panties and somehow slip them to my man when I get back to the table without anyone noticing."

Dead silence. Then the eruption of laughter came from all three corners of the room. Terryn collapsed onto another of the lounge chairs while Riley clutched her belly and cried, "I gotta pee," as she ran for the stalls.

It seemed to take forever for the laughter die down. Cheyenne pushed to her feet and turned toward the mirror to check to make sure her eyeliner hadn't run or smudged since she had liter-ately laughed till she'd cried.

"I suppose I should go get the first part done." Small renewal of laughter from all. "God help me if I know how I'll manage the second part."

Then she turned into the stall closest to her. Just as she did, all three of their phones pinged an incoming message. They froze and stared at each other in panic.

"Oh shit." That was Riley, and she had her face scrunched in what kinda looked like rebellion.

"You first?" Terryn asked, looking at Shy with her teeth bared and eyes squinted like she was comically braced for an explosion.

Cheyenne looked at her phone.

"It's from Faulkner," she told them. Their silence said they'd known it would be.

"It says: 'You have not followed instructions. You took too long. Go back into the stall and look in your purse. There is a toy in there. Attach it and bring the remote along with the panties to me.'" Cheyenne couldn't bring herself to look up. "'Also take a belfie and send it to me. Immediately.'"

Shy whipped her head up in panic. "What the hell is a belfie?"

More laughter, and then Riley said, "You can see firsthand in just a second cuz it appears"—her voice went low in mock severity and she made air quotes with her fingers—"'I've interfered with a Dom and His sub.' Gah! So I now have to send a belfie too." She said it in exasperation that was tinged with that smug feeling a woman only gets from knowing the love of a good man.

Or, in her case, two good men.

"Ugh. Make that three belfies to go, please," Terryn said and tugged at her gorgeous hunter green leather dress. "Do you see how tight this dress is? Sadistic SOB knows how hard I had to fight to get this stupid cowhide on." It was tight and lovely, and fit to her sleek figure like it was sewn on. She was a goddess of the forest with her auburn locks and nude heels. And Cheyenne thought to herself that if she had a dress she looked that good in, it wouldn't matter how much trouble she went through to put it on. She'd put. It. On.

"Amen to that, sister."

It was then that she realized she said that out loud and Riley gave her a high five.

"You know he only did that because he wants to remind you of how much fun he had helping you get into that dress," Riley teased.

"Yeah, well that part was fun." She turned to Shy and opened her mouth like she was about to explain just how fun, but all three phones buzzed again and they jumped into motion.

"Wait!" Cheyenne cried out in a high panicked voice. "I still don't know what the hell a belfie is!"

"It's a selfie." Riley popped her head out of the stall she was in. "Of your butt." Then disappeared again. "Oh my goodness you guys!" she exclaimed. "This stall has a little bench and potted plant in here. Now, I know it's a beautiful restroom in a fancy hotel, but sheesh. Who wants to sit and chill in a public stall, no matter how nice a stall it is?"

Shy giggled along with the other two and

supposed she could understand why Riley hadn't elaborated further or waited around for questions. Put like that, it was kinda self-explanatory. At least now she had a name for all those ass shots—as she'd always called them—she saw everywhere.

"Great," she said as she blushed so hard her face felt like it was on fire. "Now I gotta figure out a way to take a picture of my own ass?"

"Wait." Riley called from her stall and Shy looked over and saw her phone extended in both her hands as she apparently took her own photos. "Isn't your guy still active in the military?"

"Yeah. He is." Shy knew where this was going. "But it's mostly radio silence while he's gone and I don't hear from him until he's home."

"Oh God." The quiet in the room was instant and full of compassion.

"I couldn't imagine. How terrifying." Riley's voice was soft and dripped with sincerity.

"What you must go through." Terryn's voice, too, was so earnest Cheyenne couldn't take it. She wanted to dispel the sudden solemnity that had entered their carefree laughter on this once-in-a-lifetime type of evening.

"Guys, honest," Shy hurried to reassure them. "I have a great family." It hit her anew. This over-whelming love she had for the people who'd come into her life along with Faulkner. Her *real* family. "All of our husbands are SEALs. We hold each other up and help keep the worst of the downsides of this life at bay."

She marched back to her stall—the last empty one—and prepared to put all her worries and fears away.

This was their time. Like the freaking Goonies, she was not going to let anyone or anything interfere with their time. "Thank you both for asking. God, I can't tell you what it means to me that you did. But, um...what was your point about him being military?"

"Well, even if not when he's away, haven't you sent him a belfie before?" Riley wanted to know. Shy heard only grunts and thumps from Terryn's stall and she guessed the other woman must be fighting with her dress.

"No. Not of my butt. He has a couple pictures of it"—she couldn't believe she was confessing—"but he took those himself."

"It's super easy once you get the hang of it."

"Uh," grunted Terryn, apparently still fighting with her dress. "Says the girl with an ass so round it'd make JLo jealous." There was a huge sigh, then, "Thank God. Now I can pee."

Cheyenne loved that even as she answered the

call of her bladder, Terryn was comfortable to continue talking. Like friends. Like family.

"It's trickier if you don't have as big a target." Flush. "But, it's doable. You just have to really arch your back and get good at lining up your phone when you can't see the screen. But there is the added benefit that it makes your ass look just as juicy as Riley's."

"Hey! Your ass is hot. I don't know what you're talking about," Riley declared as she exited her stall and washed her hands.

"Oh, I know," Terryn called out over the sound of the faucet. "I never said mine wasn't good—I'm actually quite fond of it myself. I just said it wasn't as round as yours and therefore, harder to belfie."

"And therefore?" Riley made a sound that was the closest thing to a chortle that Shy had ever heard. "You sound like Z when she can't switch out of lawyer mode."

"Right?" Terryn laughed too and Riley explained.

"Ziporah—Z for short—is our friend and part of our circle, I guess you could call us. She's an assistant district attorney for the city and sometimes, when she's especially overloaded with cases, it's like she doesn't know how to speak in words that have less than five syllables in them."

It made Cheyenne like her without even meeting

her, and she asked, "If she's part of your group, where is she and her significant other tonight?" And was almost a hundred percent sure she blushed so hard it could be heard in her voice. She was now commando-girl and her little lace black thong panties were in her purse. Still having no clue how she was going to slip those bad boys to Faulkner without the other Doms noticing when, apparently, they noticed *everything*.

"It's *others*, as in she is part of a triad, like I am," Riley told her. "Only with them it's two girls and one man."

"Oh."

They mistook her *oh* as a comment on the information, when in reality it was because she'd found what Dude had hidden in her purse.

"*Oh* is right," Terryn agreed with a soft wistful sigh. "Oh, if only they swung that way. Can you imagine how hot that would make their scenes, Riley?"

"Oh my God, yes." The heartfelt groan Riley made had Shy shaking her head in wonder. It was so exhilarating and somehow freeing to have not just normal sex talk, but *kinky* sex talk like it was something as commonplace as talking about what you'd had for lunch that day.

"Of course, people—and I am among them—say

the same thing about wishing your men would play together too."

"Hey," Riley protested. Shy could see her apply a fresh coat of lipstick through the crack of the stall door. "I'm among that group. Man, what I wouldn't give to lay back one night and watch them touch each other and stroke and kiss and—I'm going to stop there because they just don't go that way and alas, I must resign myself to the burden of being the *only* object of their desire." Long pause for effect. "However will I manage?"

"So anyways." Terryn seemed to be the first to snap out of the heavy sex-filled cloud that had filled their brains. Erotic images of men and women doing all sorts of things with any and all partners involved. "They couldn't be here tonight because Cami had to work and when it comes to evenings that involve gatherings of the whole circle of us, they either all come or none of them do."

"Sounds reasonable."

At the moment, though, Shy honestly couldn't have cared less. Considering she had to figure out how to attach a freaking bullet vibrator to her clit. It had little gel-like wings that made it look like a pink and purple butterfly. As she stepped into the thin elastic loops that seemed to grow from the wings, she wondered why the hell someone would bother with going to the trouble to make it look cute. If it did what it was designed to do, she was gonna love it even if it looked like Godzilla.

It took some trial and error, then some cursing when she discovered she had forgotten to switch it on. Last thing she wanted to do was dislodge it when it had taken forever to get the thing to suction in place so that it didn't either pinch or miss its target. Tricky business for any female. She was no exception.

"How you doing in there, Shy?" Terryn called out. "I'm getting orders to help you if you are stuck and tattle on you if you are stalling."

There was a snicker from Riley.

"Well, to be honest," Shy told her, "I think I'm equal parts both of those."

"Skipping right past the part where I'm supposed to tattle," Terryn called out as she walked to stand right outside Shy's stall. "What are you stuck on? How can we help?"

"All I need is the belfie now." She was having a heck of a time arching enough so she could do it.

"Hey. There is a floor-length mirror out here." Terryn told her. "Why don't you come out and use that? We can lock the door and we won't look if you are uncomfortable."

"*Oh.* Good idea," Riley told her. "So much easier."

Shy grabbed her nerve by the shirttails, stiffened her spine, and walked out into that room wearing a vibrator and no panties under her skirt. And she walked out there to take a picture of her naked ass with two other ladies in the room.

Life had just jumped the freaking rails on her.

CHAPTER 5

FAULKNER'S PHONE finally pinged an incoming message. He held up a finger as he fished it out of his pocket.

There wasn't a power on this earth strong enough to stop the hungry groan that escaped him when he saw what his girl had sent.

Cheyenne was standing in front of a full-length mirror in a lounge area done in soft rose and peach. The lighting cast Shy's exposed flesh in a rich warm tone and really bought out her lingering tan. She had her back to the mirror, was holding her skirt around her waist with one hand and her phone over her shoulder with the other.

The woman had great legs and an ass that fueled his dreams. To see them displayed so beautifully— and that he could also see her face as well—was a bonus. She looked sexy as hell, biting her lip, her eyes open wide and a little worried as she focused. With her skirt pulled up only on one side the way it was, it partially obscured one globe of that succulent flesh. The fact that he knew her well enough to know this wasn't an attempt to be peek-a-boo on purpose made it all the more alluring.

Because it only revealed *almost* everything, the sexy quota of the photo was through the roof. It did funny things to his gut that she was so eager and willing to explore this side of their nature. That she blossomed in her own feminine power as their bond grew tighter and tighter was a huge fucking turn on.

"Well, now," he said, knowing he sounded smug as hell. "Not a thing to complain about." And returned his phone to his pocket.

"God." Riley suddenly appeared again, with a flurry of dark curls, scarlet lips and a dress to match. "That took forever. Sorry to keep you men waiting, but girls gotta talk when they travel in packs."

"Yeah," Terryn agreed and took her own seat next to Brice. "It's never just about peeing."

Cheyenne slipped into her seat on his left as though she were trying to sneak in undetected, and it was all Dude could do to keep a straight face. It was adorable how embarrassed she was. And it was invigorating how willing she was to obey, regardless.

As soon as she sat, Riley and Terryn both started talking. Loud and animated at the same time. Dude —and he wasn't the only one—could tell they'd planned this. They were distracting their men so she could slip him the designated items.

Subs. How cute were they? Banded together to run interference for the newbie. He felt a whelming sense of affection for the two gorgeous women and a measure of gratitude. Anybody who looked out for his girl got high marks in his book.

"So? Brice?" Riley asked loudly, with a sweeping motion of her hands. "Where are Kent and Angie tonight again?"

Brice wiped his mouth with his napkin before answering. Dude was sure it was to mask his grin rather than wipe anything away. Couldn't blame the guy—her overacting attempt to distract him *was* pretty cute.

"Well, beautiful," he answered when he'd somewhat gotten his expression under control. "You know they aren't into BDSM. To quote Kent quoting Angie when they found out that this night was going to include play, 'You all have fun with that. We're takin' our vanilla asses to the cop banquet instead', end quote."

The entire table shared an easy laugh. It was then

that Shy made her move and clumsily dropped the remote and her thong in his lap.

He tucked the underwear in his pocket and palmed the remote in his left hand.

Then he turned it on at the same time he asked, "And what about Gage? I thought he was going to make it tonight. No way that guy isn't a Dom."

Everyone at the table pretended not to notice the way Shy jumped in her chair or the loud clatter of her spoon when she dropped it into her bowl.

"Oh. He is." This from Brice as well. "The issue there is, he's married to my baby sister. There are just some things I don't need to see, and my little Oops in full bondage is one of them."

Everyone joined in on the soft laughter. Then Cade added, "Since Brice and Oops are also my cousins, we all mostly stick to separate nights out like this. Easier and more comfortable all around that way. Evan and Gage mostly take their subs out together, while Brice and Terryn tend to come out when we do."

"Of course," Riley added, "we all get together plenty when no play is involved."

Dude was sure that was true. In any case, he had no cause to doubt it at this point. Besides, he was too focused on the woman seated next to him to care one way or the other.

His Shy was shifting in her seat and squirming like a kid on a church pew.

The thought of what was happening between her naked legs right now in this crowded restaurant was enough to make him feel drunk. The knowledge that he held the power to control her vibrator literally in the palm of his hand gave him a hard-on the likes of which he'd never known before. Fuck.

He never bargained on the biggest test of this night being his ability to wait and not just drag her back to their room before the evening even had a chance to start.

"You ladies were gone so long we took the liberty of ordering," Brice said to the table at large, then turned and laid a gentle kiss on his woman's nose. "We got you a steak, my little carnivore."

"No gloating when it gets here, you," Riley grouched in a mock-threatening voice, then turned to Dude and Shy. "She's one of those lucky girls who eats like she's a real life Lorelei Gilmore." She shot a wistful and longing look toward her friend. "It's her superpower and it is strong with this one. I wants it too."

The meal progressed much as it started—with laughter and teasing flirty banter. Dude could tell the other subs were also receiving instructions. By the time the dessert plates were cleared away and coffees were poured, the sexual undercurrent clinging to the atmosphere was so palpable it was spreading to the tables around them.

Dude wasn't the only one who noticed the couple at the table to the left discreetly groping each other when they thought no one was looking. And unless there was an echo in here, Shy wasn't the only sub with a vibrator attached somewhere. All around them, there was a hush in the air filled with longing glances, teasing touches and hot stolen kisses.

Right then, Shy's phone went off again.

Everybody froze as she pulled her phone out with hands that trembled just a little. There was no use for her to pretend that she didn't realize every single person at the table knew who the text was from or what it was about.

Dude watched as she read.

Excuse yourself to the bathroom again. Lock yourself into a stall. And come for me. You have two minutes from the time you enter the stall. If you do not come during that time frame, you are to come back to the table and let me know. There will be consequences.

Cheyenne didn't lift her head when she said in an embarrassed yet sex-drenched voice. "Excuse me. I have to go to the bathroom. Uh-um, again."

"No."

"Don't even think about it."

And, "Not a chance, Red." All were spoken simultaneously when the other two women tried to stand to accompany her again.

Dude locked gazes with Cade and gave him a brief chin lift of thanks.

"Let the little subbie take this mission solo, ladies," Cade told the others.

Shy gasped, then pushed to her feet on knees that wobbled a little.

DEEP in the underbelly of the hotel, Miguel worked steadily and fiercely. The fury of a zealot was upon him as he neither ate nor stopped for breaks. Sweat drizzled like tiny rivers of tickling, taunting death down his brow. He was terrified.

Terrified he'd fail.

Terrified he'd succeed.

"Um, shit—" Miguel wiped the sweat from his eyes on his shoulder for what felt like the millionth time. "Hail Mary. Uh, Mother of God. Um, Hallowed be Thy name." As the words fumbled to a halt, he had a flashback to the young pastor who used to come to his low-income neighborhood to take all the kids to Sunday school when Miguel was little. It didn't take Miguel or any of the other kids long to realize their parents only let them go to get them out of their hair for two hours every Sunday.

It was boring as hell. Dorky as shit too, with all the stupid songs that would get stuck in your head for days and days. Good thing he was too old for that to happen anymore.

Without realizing he was doing it, Miguel started a quiet hum beneath his breath that sounded suspiciously like "This Little Light of Mine."

He had enough C4 and dynamite to bring down the whole building. If he'd followed the instructions right. His mom had found a ton of web sites and ordered a shitload of books on how to blow crap up. She'd been smart, he told the voice in his head that whispered like a scared bitch, about the FBI tracking their online activity.

She'd ordered things like books on stump removal from their home computer or used a public library computer and ordered shit on demolishing big buildings.

She'd even ordered a bunch of workbooks like he was going to school for this crap, and made him study and take tests. Which she'd graded and everything.

Part of him wanted to complain about the fact that if she'd paid that much attention to his studies when he was still in high school, he might not have dropped out. He quickly shut that part down and told himself to focus.

His hands shook like he was Sketchy, the crackhead who lived in his apartment building, as he placed the heavy clay-like blocks of C4 and wrapped them in duct tape. Miguel told himself he only had three more to go after this. He'd already planted his wares in two different spots within the warren of tunnels below the glitzy and glamorous hotel. Each station he'd chosen was out of the way from normal employee activity. At least he hoped it was. The places were all dimly lit and dust covered, so it'd seemed unlikely to him that anyone would accidentally stumble upon them. He'd be fucked if someone did.

He tried hard to ignore the voice that said it would be the best thing that could happen.

Miguel struggled to bring back to mind all the reasons he was here. All the reasons his mother had worked so hard to send him. He mentally groped for the righteous indignation that had fueled him as he'd made his way through the building earlier. Those rages burned hot, but never for long and usually left him feeling hollow and hung over once they'd passed.

"You can do this." His frustration at his lack of focus was so great he risked speaking out loud.

Albeit in a whisper. "Stop being a pussy. Think of your brothers. Think of Ma and how hard she cried. How long she screamed. This is right." His hands steadied briefly as his mind flashed on his brother's grave. "This is the only way they will get justice."

The shaking returned because though he'd spoke them, those last words were not his. Nor had they ever been. They were his Ma's words. And he would never tell her this, but Miguel didn't believe that killing a bunch of strangers was justice for anything.

As he struggled to find the strength to overcome his doubts, Miguel thought back to the last conversation he'd had with his mother before she'd packed him up and sent him clear across the country on his own.

"I didn't raise no pussies in my house. You don't stand there and try and tell me that you're afraid to spill a little blood!" She'd paced the filthy tattered carpet of their cockroach-infested apartment, a beer in one hand and a half-gone cigarette in the other. She'd worn a tank top that had seen a few too many battles with the washing machine. The original color could have been anything from bright red to dark brown, but had then been a muddy sort of pink that seemed to leech all but the gray out of her skin. It had clung to a frame that had faded to scrawny from a once-supple figure. She'd topped off the look with white denim jeans that she refused to believe had gone out of fashion in the nineties.

His mother, Miguel had thought, had not just told him that he was a pussy if he didn't kill people.

Had she?

"Ma?" he'd asked, outraged. "What the fuck?"

"You listen to me." She'd pointed the cigarette at him in one skeletal hand. "You quit your holier than thou judginess on me. You hear me, you little som' bitch?" She had rejoiced in calling him a son of a bitch in one form or another for as long as he could remember, because she said it was not calling him anything bad. It was his father who was the bitch.

"Look around you." She'd motioned him toward the apartment's single window. It had crusted over with so much filth no one could see out of it. "I ain't messin' with your sorry ass. Go look."

When he'd pushed to his feet and stood before the window to try and see through the grime, she'd continued, and her voice grew fierce as she spoke. Filled with emotion like he had never heard from her before. "Look out there at them useless people. They are us. Broke as fuck. Dirty. Either homeless or about to be. Just takes one bad day for most of us. You know who died in that robbing your brother was a part of? Him. Him and his friends. *Only* him and his friends. You see any rich people die that day?"

She'd stuck the stogie in the corner of her lips and grabbed him by the shoulder. "No. You didn't. And you won't. *We* get murdered. Poor people get murdered and shot up every day. You hear all about it on the news. But nothing changes. Nothing stops it. You know why?" The smoke must have bothered her, because she'd grabbed what had been nothing more than a smoldering butt and went back to pointing it at him as her bloodshot eyes bored into his. "Because our deaths don't matter to the rich. Don't you see? We *gotta* do this. We gotta take some back for the underdogs! Somebody's gotta stand up and show those rich motherfuckers that they can't keep killing us. This is war now. War."

So Miguel kept working. He shoved away the fear and the doubts and told himself this was his mission and blocked out the voice that kept telling him it wasn't too late to take it all back.

CHAPTER 6

SHY FELT a current run under her skin over her entire body. The sensation was almost like an electrical stream. It made her scalp tingle, and get that glittery shimmer you feel right before you fall asleep.

Cheyenne had been turned on plenty since Faulkner had come into her life. The guy could melt her undies from a mile away. And good lord, what that man could do up close should be illegal.

Tonight, however, was all new to them. She'd known right from the beginning that he was sexually dominant. Shy hadn't really understood what that meant until she'd hit the Internet. Then she'd scared the shit out of herself. Some of the information she'd pulled up along with the photos had been nothing less than terrifying.

It all came down to trust. At least that was how

she saw it with Faulkner. She trusted him, and so far, there hadn't been one kinky thing they'd tried that hadn't blown her mind.

Shy loved his every touch and she loved the sense she got from giving up control and placing her power in his hands.

He wielded that power like a maestro and her body was his symphony.

As they'd grown closer over the years together, more familiar with each other's bodies, he'd become a master of her climaxes. Faulkner could take her from zero to screaming "O" in under a minute flat. He'd even made a sexy game of it once. Timing how long it took for him to make her come. Then he'd smiled and done it again. Then again and again.

That'd been one hell of a night.

The irony was not lost on her that he'd given her two minutes. He'd set precedence for that. During that fateful and delightful night, he taken her still-trembling fingers in his and placed them on the soaked folds between her legs.

"It's your turn," Dude had told her in his deep Dom voice that never failed to set her blood on fire. "We are at one minute. I'm going to watch you try to break my record."

Like ice water splashed onto her burning flesh, the challenge had been a shock. Touch herself in front of him? Masturbate *for real*? With him lying on his side, head propped up on his fist directly lined up with her hip? His face couldn't have been more than six inches from her crotch and she hadn't thought she could do it at first. She'd teased guys before, and run her hands over herself to tantalize, but to actually do it for real all the way to completion, with him watching? Boy, that had been a challenge.

The first minute she'd been too embarrassed to get anything accomplished other than clumsy fumbling. But Faulkner hadn't laughed or taunted or any of the crazy reactions she'd subconsciously braced for. Instead, he'd stared fixated like a hungry lion. He licked his lips as though savoring the taste of her still lingering on them.

His pleasure. His absolute absorption in her every move had been enough to rev her engines right back up. She'd come screaming before the end of the second minute.

So now, he was giving her two minutes. And she'd be damned if she wasn't going to take advantage of them.

All throughout dinner he'd tormented her with that damn remote. Turning it on while she was talking, or up just when she was taking a sip of her wine. Faulkner knew her body so well even when she was desperately trying to hide her responses and act normal, he'd shut her off every single time she'd come close to orgasm.

Cheyenne was so turned on right now she thought she might even be able to break *his* record. Wouldn't that be something?

As she stepped into the very last stall in the thankfully empty restroom, Shy hoped she did, and that it would spur him into trying to beat hers.

Cheyenne stood in the middle of her stall and turned in a little half circle as she tried to decide how she wanted to do this. It was an immaculate place, so cleanliness wasn't a concern—thank God—but she still didn't want to be sitting on the toilet to do something so delicate. It just seemed like the least sexy thing in the world to her.

All the stalls were oversized and roomy, and since this was the back one, it was even more so. There was a small round padded seat in one corner, with a potted plant on the floor next to it. For what she needed, it was perfect.

She tested the seat to make sure it was sturdy enough, then perched herself on the edge so she could recline back against the wall.

There was one slightly scary creak when she wiggled to get her skirt and body just so, and then she was set. Reclined back, with her knees spread, all Shy had to do now was the task at hand. Literally.

A little smile tugged the corners of Shy's lips at her own joke. She lightly tickled two fingers between her folds, from the drenched opening to the now slippery butterfly she was still wearing on her clit.

Shy liked the slick sensation of the thoroughly lubricated silicone, and rubbed it against herself firmly for a moment. Its slick surface slid against her already swollen, extremely sensitized clit, and that alone almost did her in.

She'd been about to glide her fingers under the toy to take care of business, but she'd inadvertently found the button on the bullet and it roared to life with a low, purely satisfying buzz. Shy's eyes closed on a groan of pleasure. She pressed that button a second time, and a third. The vibrations got faster and more intense.

"Oh God," she gasped out. The feeling so pleasurable it bordered on too much.

Every muscle in her body tightened. Shy bit her lip. Weight gathered in her belly and lower. Cheyenne's legs began to tremble, and forgetting about her fancy 'do, she shoved a hand in her hair to clench a fistful. *Almost there,* her body seemed to say. *Almost...there.*

She was full-on squirming now, her feet doing a slow pedal on the floor while she rode the waves of her body's response. The back of her head pressed hard to the wall as a sharp spike of pleasure jolted up from her core and pulsed in her heavy breasts. It built and built until Shy feared the tension would never break and she was going to run out of time.

Then, almost unexpectedly, the pressure broke. Like the ocean's unpredictable tides, her orgasm swooped her up on a massive wave of feeling, then unceremoniously dropped her into a free-fall where for an infinite moment, she hung suspended. Even breathing was beyond her.

When the crash came, it was like that iconic moment in *Flashdance*. The orgasm fell upon her like an endless cascade of water gushing over her arched and straining form while she forgot about being still or even quiet. All she could do, all she could fathom, was a pleasure so intense she could neither control it nor contain it. Only survive it.

The buzz of her phone jarred Cheyenne out of the post-climactic haze. She groped for her purse like a drunk frat boy trying to cop a feel. Shy almost succeeded in shoving it to the floor before she managed to fish it out.

Time's up.

Shy smiled like a sap and even brushed her fingers over the simple words. She felt connected to him in this moment, regardless of the fact that he wasn't with her.

"Good gravy, Cheyenne," she whispered to herself. "You got it bad. Good thing too, cuz he's got it just as bad for you."

After mopping herself up with some tissues, Shy righted her dress and headed out. A stop at the sink to wash up had her feeling so smug she shot herself a sassy wink.

Her cheeks were flushed with rosy color. Her lipstick was gone, but her lips were plumped up from her biting on them all night. Cheyenne pulled out her little tube of cherry coke lip balm and added the gloss, so now they looked even better. Faulkner was gonna go mad—cherry coke was his favorite.

Her eyes were glassy and shining and even though she'd done a number on her hair, she thought it actually looked better now. More authentically tousled now.

She took one last second to adjust her clothing and make sure her breasts were in the right place. Since her nipples were so erect, the flimsy bra did next to nothing to hide them and the last thing she needed was to walk out there with one pointed north and one pointed west. Nothing like getting a glance at your reflection in public only to see your chest all cockeyed.

Not tonight, thank you.

Shy wasn't sure what she'd thought her feelings would be after she was finished with her mission. Embarrassed, maybe, or self-conscious? She sure as heck hadn't expected the triumphant and smug satisfaction she was experiencing.

Powerful was what she felt. Sensual and womanly and delicious. By allowing herself to be completely open and trusting, she'd opened herself to her own inner goddess.

She walked out of that restroom and to her table with a ground-eating stride that felt like the closest thing to a swagger she'd ever managed. Her strut came complete with a rolling hip sway that had men —and if her guess was right, one woman—turning to watch.

As soon as she drew near her party, she heard Cade say, "There's your alluring sub now."

As one, all heads turned. Rather than her usual fiery blush and stumble when she was the focus of too many people, she ignored all but her man and strode straight to him.

Faulkner locked eyes with her and—*swear to God* —his gaze went molten.

Fluidly, he stepped to her side and turned them both back the way she'd come, to lead them out.

His head tipped down, lips so close she swore she could feel them, he said only two words: "Good girl."

And Cheyenne felt a powerful rush. That of a sub who knew she'd pleased her Dom, and it was as addictive as crack.

She absolutely couldn't wait to see where he would take them next.

CHAPTER 7

STEPPING out into the crisp evening air, Cade breathed deep. It did less than nothing to douse the fire raging through his blood.

"Holy shit. I've missed this," Trevor, his best friend, said as he laid a brief kiss to the base of their wife's slender neck. "Too fucking long since we've taken her out to play."

"I agree with you there." Cade nodded.

Trevor held Riley's back to his chest. He had his hands on her shoulders and Cade could tell he was arching her back. The posture forced her considerable cleavage out for Cade to run his fingers over.

Everything in her stilled. He fucking loved what desire did to Riley. All the childlike wonder that allowed her to watch Disney cartoons over and over and still squeal and clap when one of them came on

TV unexpectedly dissipated like vapor when the woman put the mommy to bed. Now it was her turn.

"Would you like to play in a club tonight, Ry?" he asked, trailing his thumb between her beautiful plump mounds. "We haven't done a public scene in quite a while." He tucked the digit deep and curled the rest of his fingers over the flesh that filled his palm. And tugged. "You in the mood for an audience tonight?"

He needn't have asked. And not because she was their sub. It was that she loved public scenes. They'd discovered a few years into their marriage that public displays were one of Riley's favorite parts of the lifestyle.

It was Trevor who had a difficult time with them. Admittedly, out of the three of them, he spent the most time in the public eye, on television and as the face of his charity organization. It wasn't like he was worried people would recognize him. He couldn't have cared less about that. He simply claimed, "It was enough damn time in the spotlight."

However, when the mood struck to show off their Riley, the scenes never failed to blow not just their minds, but the mind of every person in the room.

"Yes, sir." Big eyes the color of rich amber slowly blinked up at him. She pouted a little before she lowered her inky lashes and said, "As long as Trev is doing this for himself too, and not just you and me."

It flooded his heart with a rush of warmth whenever she did that. Stuck up for Trevor. Or for him. Their Riley was wife to them both. And she stood up for each of them as fiercely as she did for their children. Even if it meant she had to step between her two Doms. Like now, when she thought Trevor was going to do something he wouldn't enjoy just to please the two of them. Or whenever Cade worked too hard, she and Trevor would literally have intervention meetings for him.

They had one hell of a woman on their hands.

"He would say something if he was uncomfortable." The lobe of her ear was soft as a whisper under the glide of his fingers. "You know him by now."

"Yeah." Trevor bit at her opposite lobe and Cade could imagine the feel of that ultra-soft flesh in his own teeth. "You know me by now."

They both pulled back as their car came forward.

The others, who'd been equally oblivious to their surroundings as they'd been, slid into the stretch SUV behind them.

Normally, the streets of the city were too congested to be reasonable for stretch cars or limos, but on the rare occasions like tonight, they were well worth the added trouble.

"Okay, I'm gonna put some stuff out there." Cade smiled at Trevor's words and shook his head as he chuckled a little. Trevor always was the first one in the pool.

"The place we are going to tonight is new to us. It's Cade's direct competition and he's been scoping it out as a possible investment."

"Yeah?" Brice asked. When Cade only nodded, he added, "Why didn't I know about this?"

"Early stages yet," Cade told him with a one-shoulder shrug. Not much else to say about it.

"No no no. Not that part," Trevor said and Cade thought he was beginning to sound like he was spending too much time having conversations with nothing but teenagers. "I only brought it up because of the point Riley made earlier this afternoon. Tell 'em what you told me, Little One."

"It's just that—" Riley had to stop and take a breath, because just then, Trevor turned on either the butt plug or the bullet attached to her clit. "Uh-hmm. That, they—um." She slapped both hands to her knees and closed her eyes for a moment. Then, her jaw clenched and she lifted her head, and Cade's shaft turned to steel at the look in her eyes.

She was *there*. Already in subspace. They'd had the toys in her belt going all throughout their meal, and the touching on the sidewalk had been intense, but too brief. She must have been aching for their play to be this far gone so soon.

Cade forced himself to unclench his muscles and relax. Well, he forced himself to *appear* relaxed, at least. They had all night and he planned on making this last.

She was too close to orgasm for speech. Trevor, of course, caught it too, and after fifteen more torturous seconds, he turned off her toy.

Her eyes clenched shut and her head dropped back. She wasn't quite able to hold back the groan that came from having her climax ripped away just when it was within reach.

"Whew," she said with a smile and rubbed her palms on her thighs. "Okay. It's just that I thought it was great timing to go to this new club tonight. Because Dude and Shy are new to all of us." She gestured toward them and shared a co-conspirator's grin with the other woman. "So this way, we will all be kinda in the same boat since none of us are familiar with this place either."

"That's very insightful of you, Riley," Faulkner told her. "It would have never occurred to me to think that having people with me who were also new would bring comfort." He shook his head. "But it does. So thank you. It makes me feel a lot more comfortable to know we won't be the only visitors."

She wiggled in her seat and smiled at him. Pouring on the coy. Yup, their sexy as hell wife was a flirt.

She was swathed in a ruby red, wraparound dress. It would only take one tug on the floppy bow at her hip for the gown to be hanging open from its three-quarter-length sleeves. All that luscious flesh beneath it on display. Cade considered it, quite seriously, and then Brice spoke.

"About that," he said, sitting forward in his seat, holding out a hand to ensure he had everyone's attention. "Just to get all the formalities out of the way before we get there." He sat with an elbow braced on one knee and pointed out each one in turn as he spoke. "Terryn's safe word is pickles"—cue surprised chuckles—"hey, you think that's bad. Hers is spinach," he told them, pointing at Riley.

"We don't really stand on protocol," Faulkner said without rancor or inflection. "Up until now, we haven't come across a situation that called for it."

The SEAL cut his eyes to his own dark-haired beauty, and the connection between them was not lost on Cade.

"But for tonight, in a public club and testing our boundaries, I think it's a good idea. You wanna pick one out, Shy?"

"Batman," she said eagerly with a little bounce.

"What? Why?" he asked on a chuckle that the whole group shared.

"Because I think it would be totally awesome to be in a club and hear somebody scream out 'Holy shit, *Batman!*' even if it has to be me."

The laughter that erupted was long and loud. Cade had tears streaming from his eyes; Trevor was clutching his gut and practically in the fetal position in his seat while Riley was laughing so hard she looked as though she couldn't breathe.

As Cade wiped the moisture from his eyes, he saw Brice holding Terryn since she'd collapsed into his lap while they roared. And best of all? Cheyenne's stoic Dom was trying to keep his cool, but his shoulders were shaking like he was having a seizure and his face was purple from holding back.

"All right then," Dude said, but he had to stop for a moment to clear his throat, having not quite gotten a handle on his mirth yet. "All right. Batman it is." He snaked a hand around the back of her neck and brought her in for a quick hard kiss. "God, you're adorable." Then he licked his lips, before diving back in for another taste. "Is that what I think it is Shy?"

She nodded, breathless, keeping her face close to his in that purely feminine way women had where their foreheads and noses touched and her sweet breath was all he could taste.

Yeah, Cade thought again, the love between them was unmistakable.

"Cherry coke," she whispered.

"My favorite," he whispered back, and cupped her jaw.

"I know." She turned to kiss his palm before resting her cheek there briefly.

The car came to a stop but nobody made a move to go.

"For starters," Faulkner said, "you and me, we're just going to find us a table where we can get a good view of the play area. After taking everything in for a while, we'll see which activity you most want to try. And if you are ready or not for a public scene. How's that sound?"

"Great, to be honest." She smiled on a huge exhale that indicated to Cade she'd been more nervous than she'd let on.

He was about to speak up, caution her about the importance of using her safe word even if she was just nervous or unsure of what was coming, so her Dom could be aware. But he needn't have bothered. Her Dom was on it before he could even open his mouth.

"Shy, you gotta let me in on what's going on in your head. I can't read your mind, and this is new territory for the both of us. We're a team. A unit. I depend on you to hold up your end of this bargain. Don't let me take you down a path you're not ready for."

"Okay," she said. "I promise. I'll be calling for Batman so much he might just show up."

He smiled at her attempt to tease him, then looked at the rest of them. "I think that about covers it. We're ready to go if you all are."

Inside, the club was an elegant lobby filled with over-stuffed furniture and heavy velvet drapes done in warm earth tones. A hostess greeted the group and asked them to sign in. Cade and Trevor had already gotten their temporary memberships in order, along with Riley's. Brice and Terryn had taken care of theirs, and had secured a visitor pass for Faulkner and Shy. Therefore, it was a simple matter of showing IDs, signing the guest book, and they were passing through the heavy gold curtain.

Inside was like stepping into another world. The club was already in full swing. People filled the place, dressed in club and fetish wear that ranged from peek-a-boo lingerie to silver-studded leather.

The small dance floor was packed. Bodies churned and pulsed to the deep, throbbing bass of the music pumping from the overhead speakers.

Everything was wood. Deep, gorgeous and golden, polished until it looked as lustrous as stained glass. All the time he and Trevor spent on building projects for their charity endeavors had given Cade an eye for lumber. He recognized the quality in the Douglas fir and knotty pine—the latter clearly chosen for its beauty. Whoever had built this place was a true craftsman.

Passing beyond the dance floor, they came to the public play area. Cade thought it was no accident that each section looked like barn stalls for million-dollar thoroughbreds. As they slowly walked the length of the room, it occurred to him that he wasn't surprised by the layout because the owner was an avid racing fan and owned several winning stallions. Watching a latex-adorned Mistress take a single tail to her muscled and straining sub while he gnashed at the ball gag in his mouth like a bit, it was easy for anyone to get the impression they were in a stable.

Black iron-wrought work was used flawlessly to add detail and contrast. Twists and whorls of it snaked along the dividing walls like gothic garland. Cade saw too that the black iron was also the metal used for the hooks and bondage equipment.

A hunger started making itself known in the pit of his belly as he eyed a hook and pulley system in the ceiling of one of the stalls.

"This one is ours for the evening." They stood staring at the reserved sign hanging from the burgundy velvet rope that closed off the opening. Cade slowly tilted his head to one shoulder and then the other, the crack and pop of his neck loosening his muscles for the work ahead.

It was time.

CHAPTER 8

CHEYENNE WALKED ALONGSIDE FAULKNER, feeling the very last thing she thought she'd feel her first time in a sex club. Powerful. Embarrassed, awkward and self-conscious were all things she'd felt before while fully clothed and in normal everyday situations. It seemed only natural that in this situation, with everything considered, she should be experiencing all of the above. But instead, she felt like she was the sexiest thing on two legs. Every step she took built this completely foreign yet completely welcome runway-model vibe, and she planned to bask in every moment.

"Let's take these, here," Brice said. He indicated with his chin a pair of plush-looking recliners right in front of the stall Riley and her men had just entered. Each one looked big enough to seat four and Shy could easily see herself snuggled comfortably with Dude in one of those.

"Take the one by the wall, Shy," Dude told her, and waited until she did before adding, "I'm going to get our drinks. What would you like?"

After he took her order, he offered to grab the first round for the rest of their group too. With a parting kiss that left her brain cells in meltdown, Dude turned and walked out of sight.

Shy might have been concerned that strange men would try and hit on her all alone in a place like this. In the past, Shy had a hard time standing up for herself. For others? You bet, she could stand toe to toe with the devil if it was to save someone else. She reminded herself all it took was a polite *no*—it didn't help soothe the frogs that were doing acrobatics in her tummy the second Faulkner was out of sight, though.

She needn't have wasted the energy. One man—tall, built and looking very sinister in his black leather pants and biker boots—started toward them. She'd noticed his eyes on their group when they had walked in. Shy had assumed he was watching them as a whole; it never occurred to her that he was in fact singling her out.

Until now. He walked straight toward her, his eyes never wavering from where she sat. Shy took a deep breath, sat up straight and squared her shoulders. She could do this. Tell this big, muscled, intimidating guy—who was no doubt a Dom—no.

Before meeting Faulkner she would have been invisible to men like him. She'd been so closed off to life and all its adventures. He'd opened her up to more than just kinky adventures, though. Faulkner also showed her love and compassion and what real family does for one another.

In her own family, she'd been the scapegoat, the one who never quite made the grade no matter how hard she'd tried. She was always her mother's example of what not to do. As a result, she'd often been the one to sacrifice, to give up her seat on the bus, or pass on the last piece of cake because surely, someone else would want it so they'd deserve it more.

Her thoughts drifted from there to Miguel Delgado, as they often did these days. She couldn't say exactly why he was never far from her thoughts. Maybe it was because she saw so much of her old self in him. The way he too seemed to be always in the shadows of his family's limelight, but she hoped that one day, he'd find the strength and freedom that she had now.

Her strength came from loving a man who truly valued her and taught her to value herself. Wherever

Miguel found his strength, she hoped he found it soon. Found the strength to decide that he was worth fighting for. His life was what he wanted to make out of it, not what circumstances or family said it had to be.

Just like now, with this big imposing man headed straight for her, she was no longer the invisible nobody in the corner. And she was no longer the type who couldn't stand up for herself either. If this Dom took one more step in her direction she was going to show everyone in this room just how new and improved she was.

Another deep breath. Yeah, she could do this.

Trevor, Cade and Brice turned as one from what they were doing and spoke practically in unison the moment the stranger stepped one foot past Riley's stall.

Cheyenne was a little surprised at the intimidation levels coming from all of them. They were striking and handsome as sin. Each one over six feet, built, and obviously powerful Doms. The three men she knew stood facing off with the one she didn't and it reminded her of the *Fast and Furious* movies, only the men were the cars. Muscled and sleek, the aggression and testosterone pumped off them like engines revving and roaring as they rumbled into position. Where they faced off, three to one.

"Something you need?" Trevor asked, naked from the waist up, loosely coiling a bullwhip.

"She's taken," Brice said as he kept his hands to his sides and rocked on the balls of his feet as though he was ready to spring into action.

"You want to go back the way you came." This from Cade, who stood deceptively still with his arms crossed and his feet planted firmly in the newcomer's path.

At first Shy thought the guys were overreacting, because come on, she could say no all by her little lonesome. But then the stranger did the last thing she expected—he planted his own feet and squared off with them. Shy felt her jaw drop.

"I thought in places like this everyone was thoroughly screened and safe," she leaned over and whispered to Terryn, who was watching with the same wide-eyed interest.

"It is," Terryn whispered back. "The guy was watching you like a hawk the moment you walked in the door, though. Our guys must have known he'd make a play."

"But again," Shy asked, a completely immature part of her secretly flattered to have the men stand for her, "isn't the screening process supposed to stop stuff like this from happening?"

"Well," Terryn said, stopping a moment to ponder

as the men continued to eye each other like combatants. "The screening is a good filter, but you still will get creeps. And this guy could be just a guy and not a creep. Maybe he thinks your Dom will loan you out for a scene, or that your Dom likes to share or watch, or sheesh, in this lifestyle he could be thinking anything." Terryn smiled at her and shrugged a shoulder. "Brice and the others just aren't willing to take the chance that he is a creep. That's all."

"The lil' subbie can tell me no herself." The stranger took a moment to look each of them in the eye. "Or her Dom can. But since he decided to walk away and leave her uncollared and unattended, I'm going to ask you boys to step aside."

Instead of meeting his request, the three men closed ranks and stood shoulder-to-shoulder. The cockiness in the other man's expression only intensified, transforming him from imposing to belligerent in a blink.

She'd seen firsthand what belligerence looked like up close and personal, maybe that was why Miguel had come into her thoughts. She was looking at a virtual clone of his brothers. And she was no longer embarrassed by the fact that the others were sticking up for her—she was grateful for it. Profoundly.

"She wasn't left unattended," Brice told him.

"Obviously," Cade said and gave one of those short, manly head-tilt things that seemed to indicate the three of them guarding her.

"No," the stranger said, unmoved by their show of unity. "What's obvious is that you don't know the rules in this club. All subbies left alone are up for grabs if they don't have a collar. If her Dom didn't want to share her or have her stolen right out from under his nose, then he should have left her kneeling and cuffed to her seat. Since he just walked away doing neither, I'm going to ask you gentlemen one more time to step the fuck aside."

"What a jerk," Terryn said. Loudly.

"Should I say something? I can tell him no right now and just avoid this." Now that the tension level had risen, Shy hated the thought of a confrontation on her behalf. The surprisingly pleasant feelings she'd had a moment ago had vanished as soon as she'd realized there might be a real conflict brewing. She was not going to just sit here like some empty-headed damsel in distress and let these men take a hit for her, and that was exactly what she feared was coming as her new champions faced off with Mr. Belligerence.

Shy shoved herself to her feet. Rules be damned,

she was going to put a stop to this before things got out of hand.

But just at that moment, Faulkner came back and Shy flowed back into her seat with a sigh of relief.

Not only was her Dom here now, so she was no longer unattended, but even if the D-bag wanted to push, not many men had what it took to stand toe to toe with her SEAL.

He had wine glasses in one hand for her and Terryn, two beer bottles by the necks for him and Brice in the other, and water bottles for everyone else tucked under his arm. Yet Shy knew if the situation called for it, he could take the other man down without spilling a single drop.

"Problem?" His voice was like chocolate for the ears and Cheyenne felt that electric tingle flare to life that he always evoked in her. It was like a shower of sparks in her belly.

Like most bullies, the creep had his head too far up his ass to see he wasn't getting past Brice, Cade and Trevor, but Faulkner was lethal. He was a soldier who fought to the death for his country each time he went on a mission, and it showed in every line of his body.

The other man must have seen this, thankfully, because he came to his senses and backed down. "No. No problem. You have a lovely sub. If you're open to it, I would love to f—" He stopped the F-bomb he'd been about to lob when Faulkner did no more than lift an eyebrow. "—scene with her."

"Look," Dude said and Shy smiled because she was very familiar with that *look*; somebody was about to get their ass handed to them. "I get the whole club scene has rules and shit. But here's *my* rule." Faulkner stepped into the man's personal space until they were practically nose-to-nose. What was left of the other guy's bravado disappeared in a blink. "She's mine. Anyone lays a hand on her and I'm breaking it off and shoving it up their ass for them. Now. Back the fuck off."

There was a tense silent moment where Cheyenne could see the guy consider his options. Mr. Belligerent didn't like being intimidated, and he looked as though he wanted to make some sort of stand or comment to save face. Thankfully, he finally realized there was a lot more than a bar fight in the eyes of the man staring him down, and he didn't have what it took to meet what he saw. Not even close. He turned and walked away without sparing a glance or a word for any of the others.

Nobody spoke until he was around the corner and out of sight.

"Sorry about that, Dude," Trevor said and shook out his arms like he'd held them tense for too long, then took the water bottles. "Guy was outta line. Honest, don't know how he hasn't got bounced from here. In our club, we'd've eighty-sixed his ass for a stunt like this."

Faulkner waved that off. "No need. Guys like that aren't exclusive to club life. Assholes come in every lifestyle." He handed Shy and Terryn their wine, then Brice his beer. "I will say this, though—that D-bag is a walking assault charge waiting to happen. Right, Brice?"

"Oh yeah, without a doubt," Brice agreed and took a swig from his beer. They clinked their bottles in salute, then Brice turned to look at Terryn. "Now then. Where were we?"

Twenty minutes later, Cheyenne thought she was going to die. She was on the seat in front of Faulkner, his legs on either side of her hips. The recliners were designed for two and equipped with all sorts of gadgets and brackets for restraints. Dude hadn't strapped her down though.

"I won't tie you up tonight, Shy," he'd whispered when he had her settled all snug between his legs. "You are going to be your own restraints." He'd kissed her softly. "Will you do that for me? Will you keep your hands where I want them just because it pleases me, Shy?"

"Yes, Sir." She'd never called him that. But in this

setting, on this night of exploring and discovery, the title felt right and true on her tongue.

"Mmm, I like the way that sounds," he'd hummed in between light nibbling kisses on the back of her neck. "I liked that a lot coming from you."

"I liked saying it," Shy had admitted. And she did. There was something that *clicked* when Faulkner got into Dom mode. Everything inside her just melted. All Cheyenne wanted was to follow wherever and however he led. She'd follow him into hell itself if that was what he asked of her—she trusted him that much.

And tonight had been anything but hell.

Cheyenne never really cared one way or another when it came to public displays of affection. She thought it was sweet to see an elderly couple hold hands and share a gentle peck of a kiss. And when young girls clung to their boyfriends with dreamy smiles on their faces, she'd always thought it was heartwarming—it made her feel kinda misty and wistful.

If people got carried away, she was firmly in the *if you don't like it, don't look at it* camp. Shy would always just look the other way if it was too much intimacy for her comfort.

So, with that as her frame of reference and knowing her mindset, Cheyenne was completely unprepared to discover she was a voyeur. Or at least she thought she might be after watching Riley and her men.

Sweet lord above, those three were hot.

They stood Riley at an angle so their small audience could clearly see her in profile. Cheyenne was not ashamed to admit complete and total jealousy of her remarkable ass, not to mention her other lovely curves.

Her arms were restrained separately in thin rope that Cade had wrapped around them from elbow to wrist, then looped over the middle finger of each hand until it looked as though she were wearing thick, woven fingerless gloves. Cade had strung the ends of her ropes through metal rings in the ceiling, but not right above her—they were off to her sides so she was standing straight with her arms outstretched as though waiting to embrace someone.

She had a matching set of ropes on her legs that Cade had spent the time and care to make into intricate thigh-high stockings that matched her makeshift gloves. Those were connected to floor posts that kept her legs spread almost as far as her arms.

Then Cade did something Shy had never even heard of—he tied her hair up. That long chocolate mass of curls had been gathered into one fist, then he'd bound it up like a pony tail and tied it to a rope directly above her.

Riley was wholly restrained. It was mesmerizing. And more than a little scary to Shy, but scary in a fun, rollercoaster kind of way, she thought. It was the most erotically beautiful and intriguing thing she thought she'd ever seen.

Then they dimmed the lights and brought out a neon tube.

"Know what that is, Shy?" Faulkner whispered in her ear. "It's called a violet wand. Looks like we are in for a light show."

"Light show?" Cheyenne was confused and more than a tiny bit concerned for her new friend. "What do you mean? Is that a laser? What are they going to do? Are they going to shock her?"

Faulkner made some sort of hand motion toward the trio, then Trevor came up to them, holding a glowing neon purple tube.

"Hold out your hand, sub."

When she hesitated, Faulkner rubbed her back in a soothing circle. She recognized the gesture for what it was—an offer of comfort and a reminder that he was right here with her. She appreciated that he didn't repeat Trevor's command, but rather just gave her a nonverbal acknowledgement that he was there and everything that happened would be her choice.

She put out her hand.

Try as she might, she couldn't quite contain her shaking, nor was she able to stop herself from flinching when Trevor touched the heart-shaped tip to her palm. She yelped. But only a little and more because of what she thought she'd feel rather than how it actually felt.

"God, that scared me spitless for a second there." Cheyenne laughed as she ran her fingers over the smooth cool cylinder of hazy purple light. "Does it vibrate or get hot or something?" It wasn't zapping her as she'd feared so unless it did something else, she couldn't see the toy offering anything more than a pretty visual.

"No. It won't get hot or vibrate." Trevor had a smirk that he didn't try to hide.

Smartass was laughing at her, Shy thought, but he was so charming and there wasn't a hint of malice in his expression, so she smirked back and demanded. "Well, what does it do then?" She added an elbow jab to Dude's ribs when she felt his body shake as he chuckled. "No laughing at me, *Sir*. I don't get it."

"I ain't laughing at you, Shy," he assured her even as he continued to chuckle. She turned enough to give him her best squinty-eyed look. "I'm enjoying the hell out of you, is all. And keep giving me those fucking cute dirty looks and we're gonna explore the spanking bench before we leave."

That wiped the glare off her face in a blink. Then Trevor spoke again so she turned back to him to pay attention.

"The electrical current runs continuously through the tool, but if I touch you with it"—he did and she felt nothing—"you can't feel anything. But watch what happens when I raise it up a bit." He lifted the wand less than an inch from her hand and a tiny purple lightning bolt zapped from it to her palm.

She yelped and jumped again, but this time when Faulkner chuckled she retaliated by wiggling her ass against where he was hard and aching for her. When his chuckle melted into a groan she said, "Serves you right," then turned her attention back to the impromptu lesson.

"There are different wands and with each you can adjust the strength of the zap it gives. We are gonna play with these a bit first and then it'll get really interesting." He turned his sandy head and pointed toward the stall where Cade was making minute adjustments to Riley's bindings. "The reason we reserved this station is because it's the last stall in the place so it's nice and dark. Also, just wait until we use the displacement mat." When he saw her brows shoot up, he answered her question before she could ask it. "It's a rubber mat that we are putting under her feet and then this"—he held up the wand—"is going under the mat. That will make her the wand, in a manner of speaking. Then, when we run our hands or tools over her, the sparks will literally fly." He winked at his own pun and walked back to where Cade and Riley were waiting to begin.

For endless minutes, they took turns running different shaped and colored wands over their beautifully tied sub. Sparks danced over her skin in a miniature ballet of light.

Cheyenne was mesmerized. It wasn't long before Riley's gorgeous body was covered in a sheen of dewy perspiration that made her skin glisten like she'd been coated with oil.

With her limbs completely restrained, Riley let her reactions out in the only way left for her—vocally. Shy watched the other woman moan and pant and beg. When the intensity increased, Riley began to shout and bite back screams. Screams of pleasure and screams of torment that were barely choked off as her men danced Riley right to the edge of her endurance, then kept her there.

The sadistic Doms withheld permission to come.

Cheyenne didn't know how Riley could stand it. She was only watching and Cheyenne was practically ready to come herself. Shy could not imagine how much noise she'd make if she were in Riley's place.

There was something so elemental about the scene. Primal. The sparks danced over her caramel skin, leaving goose bumps in their wake. Riley arched within her restraints and set her perfect rear to jiggling every time she did.

Cheyenne wasn't aware that every arch and flinch that Riley made was replicated by her own body. She didn't know she was grinding against the butterfly still between her thighs until Faulkner switched it back on. Her shout was every bit as guttural as one of Riley's.

"I don't want you to come until I give you permission." That stopped all her restless movements and she peeled her eyes away from the mesmerizing scene to meet Faulkner's intense gaze. "Will you do that for me, Shy? Fight your body and don't come until I say so?"

It was an intriguing concept. As a woman who never had much luck in the bedroom before Faulkner had come along, orgasms had been few and far between. She'd always worked as hard as she could to achieve climax, and now she was faced with denying it? Could she hold back? Was it possible for her to not come when the orgasm was upon her? She had no idea. But she thought it sure would be fun to find out.

"I can try," she told him.

He was quiet for a moment and Cheyenne watched as his eyes ran over her face like he was memorizing it. "I'm a fucking lucky bastard, Shy. You know that? Luckiest son of a bitch on the planet." Then his hand scooped the back of her neck and he pulled her in for a kiss that had her trying to climb him like a jungle gym.

"Mmm, God, babe," he murmured into her mouth as his hands molded over her curves with an urgency that matched her own. "Enough now or I'm gonna take you right here."

"Okay," she told him. After all, it sounded like a great idea to her.

"Brat," he said with an affectionate rumble. "I'm not ready to go there yet. Now turn around and behave." He thwarted his own order, though, by smashing her close for a ferocious kiss while his hands ground her hips against his, effectively reducing her mental capacity to that of a gnat.

She hadn't even realized she was straddling him until he abruptly pulled back and held her at arm's length. The molten stare they shared in that suspended moment probably raised the temperature in the room by twenty degrees.

"Sweet Christ."

She couldn't have put it better herself, she thought when the moment passed and he helped her settle back into place. His shaft was like a branding iron along the crease of her ass. Shy couldn't stop the pump and flex of her hips, but to be honest, she didn't really try.

A shout from Riley turned Cheyenne's attention back to the scene and she felt her mouth drop open. They had moved on to the floor mat portion of the show, apparently, because now neither man held a wand and were using their hands on her instead. Riley was a living lightning rod. Everywhere the two striking men moved their hands over her, sparks sizzled and zapped. Cade got down on one knee where his face was level with her navel. The way their chair was angled allowed Cheyenne to see the front of Riley clearly if she craned her neck just a little. It wasn't until Cade lowered his head and she almost fell off Dude's lap that she realized she was maybe craning too hard.

Shy watched with her breath held as the tip of Cade's tongue got closer and closer to the flesh between Riley's legs. Closer and she could hear Riley whimper. Closer still and now she heard Riley pleading. Closer, and then it happened. A hazy pink arc flashed right onto her swollen and wet clit. The breath Shy had been holding released on a gust as Riley's body stiffened and her cries filled the room. God, she was begging now. Seriously begging. To come.

"Please," she pleaded in a voice that had gone all sexy and husky, and Shy had a distracted moment to wonder if she herself ever sounded that hot. "Cade! God! Cade, please. Please let me come."

Then Trevor picked up what looked like a steel wool pot scrubber and brought it to Riley's breast. A shower of sparks erupted like a Fourth of July sparkler between it and her dusky nipple. The arch of her back and the primitive sound that emitted from her were a clear and unmistakable signal. Riley was ready. Shy knew it before she saw the men move into action.

Trevor slammed off the switch to the violet wand while Cade made short quick work of the ties. He left her limbs covered in rope and only bothered himself with the ends that were keeping his sub in place. By the time he finished her legs and was untying her arms, Trevor had her hair free. Then the two men stepped to either side of their wife.

Though they had stripped their sub bare for the scene, they had only removed their shirts. Even now

Cheyenne could see all they did was open their flies before they put on condoms. Then Trevor picked up his wife with her knees hooked over his elbows, and Cheyenne watched, entranced as he lowered her onto his cock.

It was the most shocking thing Cheyenne had ever seen. Until Cade stepped up behind her and slid into Riley's ass. His hand looked so dark and strong on the tan globe as he squeezed one supple cheek and lifted it back to allow deeper penetration.

Every bone and muscle in Cheyenne's body melted. She felt instantly drunk, so much so that she looked at her glass and was surprised to see she'd hardly touched it.

Right now, though, the only thing Shy could do was watch. Spellbound. The men were beautiful specimens of the male form. Both over six feet, thick in the shoulders with strong legs and arms. One was sandy haired and had an Indiana Jones kind of charm, while the other had the dark hair and blue eyes that reminded her of Gypsies or dashing pirates. And they stood there, toe to toe with an equally beautiful and naked woman between them.

They worshiped her with their bodies, mouths and hands. *And the sounds!* Sweet merciful heavens, the sounds they made were a concerto of sex. The wet slap of Riley's pussy as Trevor slid in and out.

The fleshy slap of his hips as Cade pumped into her ass. The way she whimpered and moaned and begged while the men growled and rumbled out praises to her littered with profanity.

"Oh fuck me, Little One," Trevor groaned. "Fucking beautiful."

The primal endearments reminded Shy of Faulkner when he got in the mood for the rougher, darker side of sex, and God how she loved it when that happened.

Cade grabbed a fistful of Riley's dark locks and craned her head back. Cheyenne gasped as he laid his teeth into her shoulder and bit. Hard. Was it the barn-like setting that had Shy thinking of stallions and mares and their primal mating habits? His free hand squeezed on one perfect breast while Trevor widened her legs even further and let his hips fly.

They were going to come. They had to, Cheyenne thought. No one could withstand that level of passion for this long and not succumb.

As if summoned by her thoughts, that now familiar weight in her belly set off a warning bell in Cheyenne's sex-drugged thoughts. She was getting close. Her hips flexed and she squeezed her thighs together to increase the friction of the butterfly on her clit. So close. Faster now, she flexed faster, and without knowing it, her hips mirrored the tempo of the scene in front of her.

Riley stiffened and arched. So did Shy.

"I'm coming!" Riley shouted it in panic. "Please. Please. May I come?"

Yes. Cheyenne thought. *God yes, please let her come.*

"Yes," she heard one of them rumble. "Come, baby. Come for us."

Riley let out a squeak and then her entire body locked and Cheyenne knew the crash was upon her. Her own breath caught, her pulsing movements froze, and that weight within her grew and bloomed and—

"Not you, Shy." Faulkner slid one hand between her legs and one to the pebbled nipple of her left breast. "You don't have permission to come yet."

The sadist plucked at her breast even as he tapped on the vibrator covering her clit. Cheyenne's vision went blurry. She arched and bit her lip in an effort to hold back. The men in front of her let loose with hoarse cries as they succumbed to their own climaxes and the sound, the sight, only served to drive her even higher.

Shy was pushing back against Dude now, her body pressing into his as she fought like hell to hold off. His hands weren't making it an easy task however.

"Oh Christ," she grit out between clenched teeth. "Please. I c-can't! I can't stop-stop it. I'm com—"

"No, baby." His voice was dark and deep and so fucking sexy she could hardly stand it. "Wait."

Then he slid his hand under her skirt and two thick fingers filled her aching, dripping sheath.

That was it. Nothing could have stopped the avalanche that was her orgasm at that point. With a scream that was unlike any sound she'd ever made before, Cheyenne's entire body arched and shook as she erupted.

"Oh *fuck yes!*" Faulkner's voice barely registered over the thunderous roaring in her ears. He banded his free arm around her and pulled her even closer. Then those magic fingers pumped faster in and out of her while he used his thumb to rub the butterfly hard against her throbbing clit. It was unlike anything she could ever remember feeling. Then another spellbinding, mind-blowing orgasm slammed into her before the first one even faded. She screamed. Faulkner growled something unintelligible and shifted them yet again.

Now he stood over her sprawled in the chair and his hand fucked her pussy relentlessly. Her legs trembled uncontrollably, her eyes watered, and Cheyenne's vision started to go cloudy as she felt yet another peak layer right on top of the others.

"I can't stop!" she gasped, her whole body felt infused with drugging pleasure. "It won't—stop—coming—"

Dude placed one hand on her throat. And squeezed. "Don't stop, Shy. Don't you dare fucking stop." The fingers inside her flipped, then instead of in and out he was pumping up and down, massaging her G-spot with pinpoint accuracy while he started to restrict her airflow.

They'd never tried breath play before, but Shy was too far gone to be panicked. No, she was amazed. Everything built within her. The tension, the pleasure, everything was heightened by the new technique. Combined with what he was doing with his other hand and the look of complete and total absorption on his gorgeous face as he mastered her body, Cheyenne was lost.

On a final gasp and shout, Shy fell into a bottomless well of pleasure the likes of which she'd never known existed and came screaming, with a rush of fluid that splashed over Faulkner's pumping hand like a geyser.

SUBSPACE.

Faulkner had heard about it obviously, but to see it in reality on the love of his life was a joy so complete and eutrophic it was bordering on hallu-cinogenic. He was hyper-aware of her and their surroundings. The beat of Shy's heart was the metronome that set the rhythm for his own.

She was breathtaking in her passion. Dark mussed hair framed her flushed face, making the porcelain beauty of her complexion all the more alluring. She was still fully clothed and though he would have loved to have her gorgeous body revealed to him, the sexy dress was an added tease. It was a dark thrill knowing the only thing under it was a vibrator and her naked flesh.

He used his hands now more to soothe than arouse, as he ran them over her still-trembling form.

Faulkner heard the soft tread of steps approaching from behind and had an insane urge to bare his teeth at whoever dared to interrupt him.

"For your sub." Brice held out a bottle of water in one hand and a soft-looking towel in the other. "She's bound to be dehydrated after that. Fucking beautiful scene, man."

Brice had the same fire burning in his eyes that Faulkner felt burning inside himself. Turning his head slightly, he saw that Terryn was in pretty much the same shape as Cheyenne.

"Thanks," he said, taking the items from him. "Your sub looks like she's there too."

"Yeah," Brice replied a little boastfully. "She shot up there pretty quick once we had two scenes to watch."

"Nice." Dude felt not a small dose of pride in his Cheyenne. Her first time in a club and she'd opened herself so completely to him and the experience that she'd not only been able to come, but she'd had multiple climaxes followed by a G-spot orgasm and subspace.

It took an insane amount of trust to let go like that in any situation, but in a public setting, it was remarkable for a newbie to the lifestyle.

"I think I'm going to take my sub to explore the spanking bench before we head out." At her hoarse gasp, Dude winked at Brice before forcing a stern expression on his face and turning to Shy. "You came before you had permission. And while you came beautifully and that pleased me very much, you will still face the consequences." Then he kissed her on the nose.

Dude scooped his subbie up and carried her to the spanking bench they'd passed on their way in. Not that she couldn't walk, but Shy was deep in subspace now and she was an irresistible armful of soft snuggling woman. He was not ready to let go.

The spanking bench was thickly padded in bold red leather. "Here you go, Shy. Careful, kneel on it here. That's the way, now just fold forward. Further, a bit more. Can you grab the handles on the sides? You see 'em? There, yes. Perfect." The positioning of the bench had her looking like a jockey stretched over a steed. Faulkner enjoyed the view from all angles, then squatted down until he could look Shy in the eye. "I need to hear your words, Shy. Time to check in."

"M'kay," she replied like a drunk at a frat party.

"Are you comfortable? Nothing pinching or poking?"

"I'm com'ferble."

Dude smiled. "What about the scene? You ready for this?"

"Hmm-mmm." Eyes that had the power to bring him to his knees were closed at the moment, so he tapped lightly on the tip of her nose.

"Words, baby. You know I need your words."

"I'm ready," she purred, then those eyes opened and what he saw in them reignited the raging desire that he had yet to quench. "Bring it."

Dude didn't trust himself to talk. Her trust, her surrender was enough of an aphrodisiac as it was. For her to throw in that ballsy spunky challenge tested his control like nothing else could have.

Dude rose and got into position behind her kneeling form, lifted the skirt and folded it over her back so her luscious ass was revealed in all its glory.

He took a few moments to run his hands over the soft globes before he began. A quick, firm massage to awaken the nerves just below the surface, with some squeezing and jiggling thrown in for nothing more than the pleasure it brought him to touch her.

He knew the others in their party had formed a semi-circle to watch, along with several club members. They all faded to the edge of his consciousness. Too many years in the military under his belt to allow him to ever completely close out his surroundings, but this was as close as he'd ever come to it. There was nothing in the world but him and his woman and the gift of her submission.

Slap. The first strike was light, just enough for a surface sting and to deepen the flush that his massage had started. Shy was so lost in the clouds of subspace that her only response was a purr. He swatted the other cheek next, a little harder, and she only purred louder.

Smack! Whack!

Two sharp blows came next, fast, one after the other, and her purr morphed to a moan. Dude, emboldened by her obvious enjoyment, struck harder and faster. Her supple flesh blossomed with color and the way her ass jiggled under the impact of the blows was a thing of beauty.

With one hand, Dude reached between her legs and double checked the positioning of the butterfly just to make sure it was where it needed to be, then he flipped it on.

Cheyenne went nuts.

Her cries rang out with delighted ecstasy as the dual sensations catapulted her right back into delirium. Dude readied himself, opening his fly and fitting on the damned condom since it was a club rule and, at last, stood behind his sub. He watched as he rubbed the engorged head of his shaft over her folds, each stroke from it bringing a plea for more from her lips.

She was pushing back into him and begging now, her cries frantic with need. "Please. Faulkner, God, please. Now. Now, oh God, now!"

And he was lost.

Sinking into her was like falling into heaven. Only, heaven could never be this decadent, this carnal. His body roared with the need for release and the raw animal hunger that clawed at him like a beast trying to get free snapped his fucking leash and ravished.

Dude's hips bucked against the cheeks he'd reddened, the globes as fiery as she was on the inside. Dude wasn't the vocal type typically but there was no holding back tonight as Shy met him lunge for lunge and stroke for stroke. Fucking him back with all the crazed passion he was fucking her.

He was going to lose it. Lose it now, and he didn't want to reach the end without her. Dude bent forward and wrapped her dark hair in his fist. With a tug he brought her head back until she was arched for him, and the angle pressed her hips hard against the vibe. With every thrust, she jolted from the dual impact and after five, soul-freeing pumps, she flew. Shy's screams fell soundlessly from her open and gasping mouth. The orgasm so powerful she went silent as Dude felt her pussy clamp on to him like it had teeth.

He didn't just *come*—she fucking *took* his climax. The force of hers ripped it from his body so there was no control. No holding back or holding anything in.

He laid his soul bare for her and with his entire being caught in the grips of it, flooded into her the most powerful release of his life.

CHAPTER 9

THE NEXT MORNING, Shy was having brunch with Riley and Terryn as promised. They'd taken her to a lovely café with a view of Central Park. It was a bit of a challenge to stay focused on the conversation, as Shy was still reeling from the events of the night before.

She remembered how she'd lain sprawled in that sex chair, floating in a cloud of iridescence unlike she'd ever known. She had gazed up at Faulkner in wonder. The ferocity of passion in his face was a sight she wouldn't forget. He'd demolished every inhibition she'd ever held and laid her soul bare to him with that scene.

Even though her head felt stuffed with cotton, and ears rang like Christmas bells, Cheyenne had still heard Dude say she was getting spanked loud and clear.

The scene that followed, her first spanking and their first public sex, had been the darkest of fantasies come to life. It had been heaven. After they'd left, she'd not believed he could possibly have another round in him. Her husband had other ideas though—they had not included more time in the club however.

He had bundled her up and carried her out with hardly more than a word to their new friends. They said their goodbyes in the lobby and took their own cab back to the hotel. Riley and Terryn both promised to see her bright and early for their siege on the city before she'd been whisked away, though.

Faulkner hadn't been through with her that night. Not by a long shot. In the cab, he'd leaned close and whispered instructions to her that gave new life to the embers of desire she was sure would have been beyond her at that point.

She should have known better. When it came to her SEAL, more than enough was just where he warmed up.

"Shy," he'd said. "When the car stops, I want you to head straight to our room. I'm going to hit the lounge and order one drink before heading up." He'd taken her chin in his hand as if he hadn't already had her full attention. "When I get to the room, I want you naked and on your back on the bed. Arms and legs spread for me. And Shy, I want you blindfolded."

Cheyenne sipped her sweet tea with lemon and sighed like a dreamy schoolgirl as she remembered what had happened next. The hurried walk through the lobby—

"Wait." Something flashed in her mind that stopped her steamy thoughts in their tracks.

"What's up, honey?" Riley asked from across the table. Cheyenne met her politely inquisitive expression.

"Oh, sorry. I didn't mean to interrupt and say that out loud," she said as she realized she had cut Terryn off in the middle of a story about some of the kids from the shelter.

"Oh, don't worry about it." Terryn waved off her apology. "It's just shop talk anyway. What were you going to say?"

"You know how sometimes you can see something, and exactly *what* you saw won't register until much later?" When the other girls nodded she continued. "Well, I just remembered my walk through the lobby last night when we got back to our hotel." Cheyenne squinted and rested her forehead in her hands as she tried harder to focus. "But I *couldn't* have. That just can't be right."

"Cheyenne?" Terryn asked, concern in her voice. "What? The suspense is killing us."

"It's the damnedest thing." She plopped her hands on the table and looked into the faces of her new friends. "I must be going crazy, but I could swear I saw someone from home by the elevators last night."

"They were probably just on vacation too," Riley told her and took a bite of her Cobb salad. "This is New York City, after all. The place is crazy with tourists."

"Yeah, I know that and maybe I'm wrong," she said, even as certainty settled like a lead ball in her gut.

"But you don't look like you believe that," Terryn told her and placed her hand over Cheyenne's.

"To be honest, no. I don't believe I'm wrong. The problem is I can't shake the feeling that there is a reason he's here." She took another sip of her tea and it felt like she'd swallowed sand instead of liquid, thanks to the choking fear that had grabbed hold of her. "A not good reason either. You guys know how Faulkner and I met, right?" When the others nodded she went on. "Well, during the rescue, the guys holding us hostage were all shot down by the SWAT team. Then a few months later, the brother of one of those men and the sister of another got together and kidnapped me again."

The others gasped and offered words of shock and concern, but she waved those away with a smile of thanks and went on. "It was somehow their twisted sense of revenge." Riley and Terryn both reached out in comfort again, but Shy was quick to assure them. "No. No, I'm fine. It's all water under the bridge and Faulkner saved me that time too. So, it's all good."

"Is the person you saw one of those last two who attacked you? Aren't they in jail?" Terryn looked outraged at the possibility that they were free.

"No, those two are in jail and won't be coming out any time soon. It was Miguel, the third brother. I would know him anywhere." When the other two looked a little confused, she clarified. "I couldn't help but watch every interview and show the families of those who attacked us appeared on," she admitted, feeling sheepish. "After it happened, the reporters were relentless, and when neither Dude nor I would give interviews, they just twisted the story around to police brutality and made the whole world feel sorry for the men who tried to blow me up."

"That's just bullshit."

"I know, right?" It felt incredible to have their instant and unwavering support. "It was so hard for a while there. Even my own mother and sister believed the reports and took their side against me."

More shock and outrage, and Cheyenne couldn't have put into words what their reaction meant to her or how it helped fill in the hole her family left behind. "But, I still watched every clip and exposé and that's how come I recognized Miguel. He was just starting high school so the reporters really pushed on how he lost his 'father figure' so violently and tragically." Remembering it that way pulled at her heartstrings for the poor kid all over again.

"Psssh!" Riley had a look of disgust on her face. "Seriously? Some cretin straps a *bomb* to you and the media is worried about someone losing him as a father figure? Yeah. That sounds like the father of the year to me. What about you, Terryn?"

"Oh yeah." The sarcasm Terryn loosed was sharp enough to cut. "If only Brice would be as good of a father."

"Oh wow. You guys are awesome." Cheyenne felt close to these women after their shared night of passion. Maybe for people used to the BDSM scene, nights like that would be no biggie, but to her, it had been life-changing and these women had been an integral part of it. They mattered. Their support mattered.

"I get it, and I couldn't agree more that he had to have been a terrible influence. My question is, why is Miguel here? That's what's got me worried. I don't mean to be all over-dramatic and woe is me, but am I crazy to think him being here when we are is more than just a coincidence?"

"You don't think he's going to try and uphold his family's legacy do you?" Riley's eyes got huge in her pretty face as the worry that Cheyenne was feeling seemed to settle in her gut.

"I don't know, but…" Terryn fished in her purse and came out with her cellphone. "I think we need to let Brice and Kent know just in case."

"I hope to God we are overreacting." Cheyenne pulled out her own cell and called Faulkner.

Overreaction or not, she knew she'd feel better once she talked the whole thing through with him.

CHAPTER 10

FAULKNER HUNG up his cell slowly and with great care. He felt old, as if the last five minutes had aged him a dozen years. Miguel Delgado in New York City and at their hotel. It had to mean bad news for everyone involved. After Shy's call he'd immediately contacted Wolf, the first one of his SEAL team that came to Dude's mind in a situation like this. Less than two minutes and Wolf had confirmed one thing; Miguel was not in Riverside.

It was enough for Faulkner to be convinced.

With a groan, he leaned his back against the wall for support and barely registered the bump when his head met drywall with a loud crack.

"Faulkner." Brice Marshall came toward him in a ground-eating stride and there was urgency in every line of his impressive build. "I just got off the phone with Terryn. Did Cheyenne get a hold of you yet?"

The halls were filled to bursting with both on- and off-duty police, as well as other people in law enforcement for the convention.

"Yeah. She just called," he answered as the most likely reason for Miguel's presence here settled in his gut like a cancer. "He's going to blow up the hotel, Brice." Faulkner felt the weight of certainty settle on his shoulders like a hundred pounds as the muted rumble of over a thousand law enforcement officers echoed in his ears. "We gotta evacuate and sweep the building."

Brice looked as concerned as Faulkner felt, which he appreciated because at a time like this, the last thing he needed was a Doubting Thomas slowing up what needed to be done.

"All right." Brice checked his watch. "My captain just started his lecture in the Liberty conference room in the west tower. He should be wrapped up in an hour. Maybe we get an additional fifteen minutes after for Q and A. But no more." He stepped closer when a group of uniformed cops poured into the hallway from a nearby elevator. "That doesn't give us a helluva lotta time. We gotta either find the kid or find the bombs before he's free. Because no way in hell is the captain going to okay an evac on 'I think I saw someone who might be'. No way in hell."

"Dammit." Faulkner knew Brice was right. No one in their right mind would take such drastic measures on what amounted to nothing more than a hunch. It didn't change the fact that he knew he was right though. Not one bit.

"All right. Kid's in the system already. Think you can arrange to get his mug shot passed around here? Maybe get the hotel to print it up for us at the desk?"

Brice nodded as he worked his cell. "Already on it. What else you need?"

"I'm going to hit the laundry rooms, storage rooms and the like to start looking for bombs."

"Great. I'm going to snag Kent and a couple guys from my squad. We'll start looking for witnesses and we'll look for anything that might be planted up here while we're at it."

"Perfect." Faulkner stood and extended his hand, and the two clasped in a firm grip of unity. "Do me a solid. Tell your women to keep Shy the hell away from here until they get the all clear from us. That woman is hell-bent on getting herself blown up in these situations."

"No shit? Yeah, my Red put herself in harm's way before. Once. About killed me," Brice said, and from his expression, Faulkner knew he understood the soul-wrenching fear that only happened when the love of your life was in danger.

"Yeah," Dude said. "I like her all in one piece though, selfish bastard that I am. So I'd like to keep her as far away from here as possible."

"I second that. In fact, I'll text the whole crew and make sure they all steer clear till this is settled."

Faulkner was relieved to see he was true to his word as Brice was already tapping away on his phone before he'd turned to leave.

He knew he should call Cheyenne and keep her in the loop on what was happening. If Faulkner believed she'd do nothing with that information and stay put, he would. However, he knew his woman, and Cheyenne was not the type to sit idle when she knew people were in danger. Especially if she thought she could help. In this case it was even worse. Faulkner knew Shy would somehow feel responsible.

She was a sensitive and empathetic person who always felt deeply for the pain of others. It was what made her such an incredible 911 operator. She put herself in everybody else's shoes and talked them through the tragedies and triumphs of their lives.

So naturally, she'd been heartbroken for the dirty,

underfed boy whose family had been literally blown apart.

Cheyenne had made several anonymous donations to a bereavement account for him until the news had broken with a story about the mother squandering all the money.

Cheyenne never quite shook the unwarranted sense of duty she'd felt for the kid and although he couldn't claim to share the feeling, Faulkner understood *her*. That was why he knew that unless the others physically prevented it, Cheyenne would show up here and try to help.

Brice said they had an hour to find proof before they went to the captain. Faulkner figured he had half that to find the kid before Shy broke away from the others and came charging in on a white horse.

"Fuck." At Brice's exclamation, Faulkner turned toward him. "They aren't answering their phones." Brice looked again at his, as though by the power of his will, he could make one of the women respond.

"I got a bad feeling about that," Faulkner told him.

"Me too." Brice spotted his partner headed their way. "Change of plans. Hold one second." Then jogged to meet him halfway.

There a brief, intense discussion that ended with

Kent bolting away while barking into his radio. Then Brice was back.

"Kent is gonna organize and start the search. Let's go find our women."

CHAPTER 11

IN AN ALLEY TWO BLOCKS OVER, Miguel threw his burner phone to the ground and smashed it with a brick—one he'd taken off the pile of trash he was hiding behind.

Tears he'd thought had run dry over the last ten hours started up again and rained down his dirt-smudged face, leaving trails in their wake.

The sharp impact when the rock hit plastic and the crunch that resulted was a relief. So he hit it again. Shards flew in all directions. One tiny sliver lodged itself in the back of his hand.

The symbolism wasn't lost on him. The complete destruction of something by the force of his actions.

So he hit again, harder, and again with a sound like a wild thing rising in his throat. Then he couldn't stop. Not the cry, nor the pounding because

Miguel knew, no matter what the outcome, he was going to die today.

"ARE you sure we should be doing this?" Terryn asked in a whisper as though their husbands might overhear them from two blocks away.

"No, I'm not sure about this at all," Cheyenne confessed. "But I do know I will go crazy if I don't at least try to help."

"I think it's good we are sneaking in through the back entrance. They're probably going to have uniforms posted at the main doors to keep people from coming in and to look out for Miguel."

"Yeah," Terryn agreed. "They would spot us for sure and then we'd get nowhere fast." She shot them both a look that made it clear she wasn't so sure that would be a bad thing. "I have to say this, guys. But are we sure that we won't be more of a hindrance than a help? We don't know how to sweep for bombs, and they are bound to be evacuating the hotel by now. I just would hate it if we were in the way and made things worse instead of better."

"I know," Cheyenne said on a gust of an exhale since she was fretting over the same thing. "You're probably right and if we get there and see that they do have everything under control, we can bail. But I just can't shake this feeling that I have to try. I know it's crazy to feel responsible for him, but now that I remembered it, I can't get Miguel's face out of my head. He looked scared, guys. He looked like he was about a million years old. If there is any way I can help him, I need to try."

She didn't voice the other reason she had to go. It was the same reason Terryn and Riley were coming with her instead of letting her go alone. Their men were in that hotel too. Trevor was there. He was going to speak about the drop in crimes committed by teens when there was a well-funded rec center in place. Even though the center was mostly run by Trevor and Riley, Cade was involved as well.

So both of Riley's men as well as Terryn's and Cheyenne's were in harm's way. Not one of them were willing to sit on the sidelines and wait like a bunch of wilting violets from a bygone era while the men they loved were in danger.

"Let's cut through here," Terryn said and headed down a particularly ominous-looking alley. "It'll be faster than trying to circle the building for the back door once we get there. We can approach from behind instead."

Ominous or not, it was a solid plan so Shy and Riley followed the redhead in.

"Oh." Riley's gasp was a soft exhale of compassion. "Poor thing."

With each step they got closer and closer to a person hiding behind a huge pile of what looked like construction rubble. Pitiful weeping and unintelligible words could be heard from that direction.

Cheyenne felt her heart clench. She was no stranger to homelessness and poverty. They had more than their fair share where she came from too. However, thanks to movies and the news, Shy had this low level but unshakable—and yes, unreasonable—fear that all homeless people in New York City were knife-wielding lunatics out to steal her shoes. Of course, she also secretly believed that sharks could get her even in swimming pools, so she kept her weird paranoia to herself.

Nevertheless, Shy felt her heart break. The pain was palpable in his soul-wrenching sobs.

Determined to walk by without drawing attention, since she was fairly confident he was back here in search of privacy, Cheyenne and the others quickened their steps. She didn't see the rebar protruding from the pile until she tripped over it.

"Son of a—"

Sharp, intense and severe pain—the likes of which only happen when you bang your shin or step on a Lego block—brought Shy to all fours. She hardly noticed when the others gathered around to check on her.

Stunned by the sharp throbbing, it took her a full thirty seconds to register that the person crying in the rubble was none other than Miguel Delgado.

CHAPTER 12

"I CAN'T DO IT." Miguel looked right at Cheyenne and felt no surprise whatsoever—it was like he'd been expecting her. "She's gonna kill me." He wiped a grimy sleeve under his runny nose like a lost and frightened kid, but he didn't see scorn on any of the faces surrounding him, like he'd expected. No, these faces showed him nothing but pity. "Aw, fuck," he amended, "she's—she's gonna hate me. But I can't do it. I c-can't."

And like the child he was, he collapsed against her chest and clung while grief and fear and sorrow poured out of him. She should hate him. They all should, for what his family had done, and for what he had set up in that building. Instead, the three women standing in that alley with him were sharing his grief, crying as they gathered close and wrapped their arms around him.

A boy who'd never known the embrace of his own mother, now in his most dire moment, found himself surrounded and embraced by three. As the years of abuse and neglect, anger and pain bled out of him like an open wound, they held him and soothed and murmured words every child should have grown up hearing, but he never had. Until now.

"It's going to be okay."

"We're here now."

"We can fix it."

"We've got you."

"You're not alone."

"Wait." Miguel moved to pull back even though he was still losing the battle for control of his tears. His small chest heaved and his bottom lip quivered as he valiantly fought for composure. "I gotta go back. You guys don't know what I did. I gotta stop it before someone gets hurt!"

Urgency and tension grew in him with each uttered word—an urgency the women seemed to share.

"Let us help," the redhead told him softly.

"I can't." A lock of lank, greasy hair fell over his eyes when he shook his head. Even as one of them brushed it back with gentle fingers, he pulled farther away. "I can't take the chance you might get hurt. Any of you."

"Miguel?" Cheyenne didn't bother to address how she knew who he was, which didn't surprise him. The situation was beyond that.

"Honey, whatever it is. We can help. You don't have to do this alone."

As he continued to shake his head and back away, Cheyenne and the others matched him step for step.

"Can you at least stop moving and tell us what is going on?" The dark-haired one spoke soothingly, as though to a toddler or a cornered animal. In his fragile state, both images fit. Then she firmed her wobbling chin as well as her voice and scolded. "We know it's probably about Cheyenne here, and probably involves bombs. Tell us now and we will help you fix this before it's too late."

Maybe it was the way she tried to sound fierce when the little brunette was anything but scary, but it worked.

"I put 'em in the hotel," he said in a quiet, shame-filled whisper. Then he took a hold of himself and squared shoulders that felt far too small for the weight of the next words he spoke. "There is one that will definitely blow when I take it out." His eyes were dry now, as he locked gazes with Cheyenne and spoke about his own death. "Will you call your husband and tell him to clear your hotel? All but one of the bombs has a basic trigger that anybody could figure out. But there's one that's foolproof. It's a small one, I thought I was being a big shot and that even if all the others came down, this one at least would kill the person disarming it." His eyes filled with tears and shame as he looked Cheyenne face to face and owned up to his actions. "I rigged it for your husband. Thought at least, no matter what, he'll die for what he did. I was so wrong. I'm so sorry, I shouldn't have even come here." He took a deep, cleansing breath. Confessing felt right, it steadied his resolve and his nerves. "I don't know for sure what kind of damage it'll make, but nobody else has to get hurt. But I'll do my best to make sure it only gets me. Just me."

"Oh no, Miguel." Cheyenne and the others surrounded him again.

He stood stoic and brave—at least that was what he intended. His violent shaking betrayed him though, broadcasting his fear in Technicolor. "Nobody is dying today. Nobody."

"You know, that's how Faulkner saved me. He can dismantle whatever you set faster and cleaner than you can imagine."

"And it's a police convention," Terryn reminded him. "Whatever poetic justice you thought you were extracting before, now that just works in our favor. The people with the know-how and experience to fix this are already there." She smiled encouragingly and gave his hair a tug.

Miguel looked from one to the other of them.

Cheyenne watched him struggle with literally life-and-death decisions. And Miguel saw pity in her expression. Not a pity that made him feel ashamed, but one that he took strength from; one that showed him there was kindness and compassion in the world. It only strengthened his resolve to do what was right.

His voice cracked and croaked when he started to talk, the pent-up emotions tangling with the words he needed to speak.

"Okay, but I still have to go. For the one that's booby-trapped." His eyes filled anew. "Not even I know how to disarm the thing. So it *has* to be me who does it. I can't stand back and let someone die because I couldn't stand up for what's right."

When his brave face crumpled to reveal the frightened child beneath, he was embraced once again.

"WHAT THE *FUCK*?" Faulkner watched in baffled disbelief as Shy, Riley and Terryn sprang apart from their huddle around Miguel. Then experienced the feeling multiply when the three of them closed ranks around the kid.

"What in the hell is going on?" He wanted to know.

"Where have you been?" Brice added for good measure.

"We can explain," Shy told him.

"It's not what you think," Riley added.

"He's just a scared kid, Brice," Terryn told her husband as he stared at them, dumbfounded.

Then Dude couldn't understand a damn word as the three women rushed to talk all at once.

Suddenly, all hell broke loose. Miguel turned and ran like he was a fucking Olympic sprinter.

"What the—?" Brice shouted. "Freeze! You little shit, get back here." And Brice bolted into pursuit.

"I can't!" Miguel yelled back as he gained distance. Just before he rounded a corner, he shouted, "I'm sorry! Get everybody outta there! I'll stop what I can. I promise." And then he flew.

No matter how hard he and Brice pumped their legs, Miguel's lead on them only grew. "Goddammit!" Brice said and grabbed Faulkner by the arm and slowed them both to a stop. "Hold up. He's gone. Let's hope the girls knew what the hell he was talking about."

They turned and Faulkner was impressed to see all three of the women had joined the impromptu race. Due to shoes chosen for fashion over speed, they were about half a block behind, but not one of them was slowing down, and all looked hell-bent on their mission.

Shy got to him first, but she was too winded to speak and stood with her hands braced on her thighs as she tried to catch her breath.

"He told us the bombs are in the boiler room and where the backup generators are," Terryn panted as she reached them and wrapped her arms around Brice for a quick but fierce hug. "The hotel needs to be cleared. He says one of the bombs is booby-trapped and it's going off no matter what."

"That's why he ran." Riley grabbed Brice's arm as tears fell unheeded down her lovely cheeks. "He says he can't let anyone die. Anyone but him."

She turned away from Brice and eyes of liquid brown locked onto Dude's. Faulkner was not immune to their impact.

"Can you help?" Riley's voice cracked as she spoke. "He said he made something that can't be defused. Do you have any SEAL tricks for a situation like this?"

"SEAL tricks?" Shy said with an eye roll. Leave it

to his Shy to bring a little light into this dark situation. "Like balance a beach ball on his nose?"

Dude kissed the top of her head and rubbed a soothing circle on her back. He knew she often used humor when she was under pressure. "She's just kidding, Ry. Bad jokes help her stay calm and keep things in perspective when she's scared. As it happens, I got a lot of tricks up my sleeve." He answered Riley while Brice argued with someone on his cell about disrupting his captain's lecture. "I'll find Miguel and his booby-trap. Then I'll do my damnedest to get us both out in one piece."

Brice hung up and put his phone back in his pocket.

"Since it's moved from hunch to fact, I went ahead and called it in. We need to move on this, now. Let's go."

Both men looked at the women.

"Don't waste time, honey. Let's walk while we talk." And Terryn was off, leaving the others with no choice but to follow. She was right—arguing would obviously get them nowhere and this was an *every second counts* situation.

CHAPTER 13

MIGUEL RAN. He didn't look back and he didn't slow down. If his hunch was right, he had about three minutes before the cops started swarming the lower levels. He didn't care about the big bombs. Those were set with basic timers and fail-safes that he knew the SEAL could probably disarm in his sleep.

The only thing he cared about—the only goal he had right now—was to get to the rigged one before someone else got there first. If that happened, that explosion itself wouldn't be strong enough to cause structural damage, but it would kill whoever was within a ten-yard radius.

It wasn't set with a timer but instead had a mechanism that would trigger when it was moved or jostled. That was why it had to be him—anybody who disturbed it would die for sure.

Just the thought turned his bowels to ice and Miguel dug deeper and ran faster than he'd ever run in his life.

DEEP in the underbelly of the hotel, Faulkner and Cheyenne ran as one. They didn't waste breath on words, just clung tight to each other's hand as they raced to stop the unthinkable before it happened.

Terryn and the rest of their group had broken away from them as soon as they'd entered the lobby. They would lead Brice and others to where Miguel said he'd hidden the other bombs.

The kid hadn't said where the rigged one was set up, but Faulkner had an idea. He'd waded into situations like this too many times to count, in circumstances more dire than this. Masterminds who ran militias and/or entire countries had set up most of those incidences. Dude got that the kid was scared and believed his detonator was un-breachable, but he'd be damned if he couldn't dismantle a rig fixed by a seventeen-year-old novice.

Down one dusty corridor to the left, then a quick pivot and they barreled down the one on the right. Left. Right. The lighting grew dimmer and the air danker the further they went.

Dude was pretty sure poor Shy was going to have

a few broken bones in her hand. He'd also come close to yanking her arm out of socket a couple times when he'd changed directions on her. Since she refused to stay away, he was keeping her glued to his side where he could assure her safety for himself.

He couldn't say he was positive where they were headed, but his years in this business gave him a better than average guess, so he was going to follow his gut, then work outward until they found what they were after.

They rounded another corner, slammed through a heavy steel door and found themselves in a dank, unfinished area with exposed beams and electrical wiring everywhere.

Dude stopped and pulled Shy close as they both panted and looked around. There were three doors leading out of this room. One had an exit sign above it, the other two were unmarked. They had a fifty-fifty chance of heading in the right direction.

Faulkner cursed under his breath and felt like laughing when his childhood drifted through his mind with the singsong "Eeny, meeny, miny, moe" skipping along his jumbled thoughts.

"Oh God, honey." Shy's grip tightened and she pointed toward a shadowed corner. "Look."

"Don't." Miguel sobbed, his arms full of what

looked like a pretty straightforward homemade boomer. "Don't come any c-c-closer!"

Tears and snot smeared his flushed face and Dude saw what Shy had seen all along—just a scared, lost kid. When he sniffled and awkwardly wiped his cheek on one bicep, Dude felt his heart twist with compassion.

"Just hold on, son," he said, lifting his hands to show one was empty and the other held Shy. The boy had nothing to fear from them. "Let me help."

"No." Frantic head shakes and more sobbing. "No. You can't. Didn't she tell you?" His swollen, tear-wrecked eyes turned toward Cheyenne for one trembling moment, then back to his with renewed desperation. "You need to get her out of here. She knows! It's gonna blow up. This one can't be stopped. I gotta get it outta here before people get hurt."

"That's not gonna happen, kid," he told him plainly. "No way in hell you're getting out of this room with that thing. Now, lay it down and step away. If it's gonna blow no matter what, we can evacuate and set it off without anybody getting hurt."

"I can't!" Miguel yelled. His voice cracked and his body quivered with the force of his conviction to right his wrongs. "Don't you listen? Don't you get it?

I have to do this! It's the only way." Hiccupping sobs shook his armful in a way that made sweat prickle on the back of Faulkner's neck.

"Enough!" Faulkner shouted. Miguel and Shy both jolted at the loud and unexpected burst. "That's not a toy you're cradling, boy. That's a fucking bomb! Now put it down, and step the hell away so I can do my fucking job."

It almost worked. For a second, his tone got through and the kid nodded his assent and bent forward as though he were about to lay his burden on the floor.

Then the unthinkable happened. Dude heard the slightly metallic snick as his bundle shifted.

"Freeze!" he shouted, but he needn't have, Miguel heard it too.

As long as Dude lived, he knew he'd never forget the look in those huge dark eyes when they met his.

He didn't have time for diplomacy and wasted none on finesse. With all his strength, he shoved Shy as hard as he could in the opposite direction and raced for the kid.

Miguel stood trembling and braced for the end, but Dude wasn't gonna let him go without a fight. With one hand, he grabbed the bomb. The other, he clamped on to the boy's collar and yanked the two apart, flinging the bomb toward the door marked exit.

White. Hot. Brilliantly bright and brutally loud, the bomb exploded with the roar of a dragon. Even as he felt the full body impact from the blast peppered with shrapnel, he wrapped his larger frame around Miguel's as they crashed to the floor in a shower of fire and smoke.

CHAPTER 14

PAIN WOULD COME, he knew, but for now there was only chaos. Silence was a deafening roar in his ears. The absence of sound thrummed though his head like a vacuum and his vision had gone psychedelic from the flash. Every movement had tracers and even the things that were stationary looked as though they pulsed and swayed.

He had to move. Shy. He had to get to Shy and make sure she was all right. The disorientation was familiar, a partner he'd waltzed with before.

Years of military training moved him now. Got his arms to release their hold on the boy and allowed him to push himself to his hands and knees over the prone body beneath him. Dude's first thought, his only thought, was Shy. He'd do what he could for Miguel once he knew she was safe.

Clouds of smoke and debris still floated in the room and the orange glare from the smoldering rubble cast the light with an eerie glow, only worsened by his still-ruined vision.

It took all his strength to push back to a kneeling position, but he made it. Just as he was trying to convince his body to get to its feet, Cheyenne stumbled to him and collapsed at his side.

"Thank God." Relief poured renewed vigor into his body and he wrapped her in his arms and clung. Dude felt her sobbing on his chest, though he still couldn't hear and pulled her in tighter. "Thank God, you're safe."

CHAPTER 15

CHEYENNE COULDN'T HEAR above the ringing in her ears. She supposed she should be grateful for the shrill sound, though a few moments ago, there hadn't even been ringing, only the strangely buzzing silence that reminded her of being underwater. Relief and pain mixed in a head-spinning brew of giddy confusion and her thoughts jumbled like the flecks in a snow globe as she held on to Faulkner and cried.

She felt the rumble in his chest that told her he was talking, although she still couldn't hear him. His big, scarred hands rubbed a soothing circle along her spine before he gripped her shoulders and pushed her back from his chest.

As soon as she was at arm's length, he started the pat down. Shy understood completely—she also had a need to ascertain for herself that he was all in one piece and free of injury, so she returned the favor. When one of her hands landed on his side just over his ribs, a jolt of panic lanced though her heart. Wet, sticky and terrifying because there was a chunk of metal sticking out of him. He flinched and stilled when she landed on it and the two of them locked eyes for a moment before they both looked down.

His maroon shirt was black with blood and stuck to his side. The black turned crimson when it ran to his jeans and Shy was alarmed at how far down the streaks already were. Gingerly, she lifted the hem of his shirt and peeled it away from his flesh as gently as possible. Her gasp and cry fell on still-deaf ears but he showed he knew her worry anyway for he brushed a calming hand over the crown of her head that seemed to say it was going to be all right.

Looking at his ruined side, a thumb-sized chunk of pipe stuck in his ribs, Cheyenne felt her stomach threaten to revolt. The wound seeped a steady flow of red and she didn't have enough medical knowledge to know how much was too much, but it horrified her. Dude grimaced and grabbed the piece between two fingers. It came free with little effort and a new rush of blood. Gruesome as it was, Shy was relieved to see it wasn't as bad as she'd first believed.

There were other wounds, as well. Gashes that ranged in size from superficial scratches and scrapes to gouges as long as her forearm. Scrambling around to check for further damage, she saw more on his back and shoulder on that side as well as several places that had already started to bruise.

The ends of his hair were the ashy brittle brown of dead leaves and there was an angry red flush to his skin from where the blast of fire singed him, but she guessed he was in pretty good shape for having just gone toe to toe with a bomb.

Cheyenne worked her way back to his front, looking for damage she might have missed, when his voice cut through and she heard him speak. "Shy. Hold still and let me check you again."

"I'm okay," she said, shaking her head and running her hands along his blood-soaked thigh. Thankfully, it seemed as if there was no other damage aside from the side of his torso that had taken the brunt of the blast.

He wasn't to be put off though, and she stopped her fussing. All it took was for her to see him flinch when she tried to keep going. She froze, and then it was his turn to examine her.

She was unhurt. There was a sting in her palms and her knees from where she'd fallen. Or, more accurately, where he'd thrown her.

Cheyenne had already been leaping away, so with the added force of his heave, she'd almost made it completely across the room before the explosion. Shy had curled into the fetal position as tight as she possibly could and covered her head.

What had happened next had been nothing but a blur of sound and heat.

She wasn't sure if Miguel intended for such a small blast from his bomb or if it had misfired somehow, but she was thankful for it all the same. Euphoric relief washed through her as the shock and adrenaline started to wear off and the realization that they had successfully stopped the bombing sank in.

Cheyenne raised her face, wanting nothing more in that moment than a kiss from Faulkner to celebrate their survival. Only, as soon as she saw his expression, all the joy she felt evaporated like mist in the sun.

He wasn't looking at her; his expression was solemn as he stared intently just over her shoulder.

"Miguel," she whispered, but Faulkner's eyes finally lowered and he met her gaze. The look in them told her she didn't want to know. She did not want to turn to the frighteningly still body of a seventeen-year-old boy and see for herself.

But that was what she did. It was what she had to do.

She cried, "No! Oh, Miguel!" And tenderly as she could, took those small shoulders in her arms and turned him. "Oh God, baby. Sweet boy. You're going to be okay, hang in there, 'kay? Stay with me." Her mouth crumpled and her chin quivered uncontrollably, making speech almost impossible.

Miguel's stomach wound made Dude's injuries look like nothing more than playground boo-boos. There was a strange hollowness to his middle that terrified her.

Adrenaline flooded anew as she prepared to wade into the battle for this child's life.

"Don't let go, baby," she told him. "You stay with me."

"Shy, sweetheart." Faulkner's voice came through. Somewhere in all the pandemonium happening inside her head, he was the calm within the storm. "Lay him back a little. Let's see. *Ah, fuck me. I'm sorry, Shy.*" His soft curse held a lifetime of experience. That experience told him when there was no hope.

And it broke her fucking heart. Her eyes snapped to him in panic and she shook her head, shaky in jerky denial.

Then she heard a tiny crackle of a voice and looked down into Miguel's pale earnest face.

"Did—they—find the—rest?" Long pauses with shallow pants in between, but she understood every word.

"Yes." She blatantly lied because she had no way to know the answer to that yet. But that didn't matter—he needed peace right now, needed to believe that he'd been able to reverse his actions and redeem himself. "All clear. You did it. You saved them." She laid a tender kiss on his too cold forehead. "You saved everybody."

His lips stretched fractionally in smile of victory. "I—couldn't—do it. I'm sorry. I never should—have come. Never wanted to but—she—made me. Said I didn't—love—love my brothers if I pussied out." He faded and seemed to wilt in her arms and she felt panic rise again. "I loved—them. I did. But s'not right. Just—not—"

Then nothing. His mouth moved in a silent gasp and suddenly it was if he weighed only half as much as he had only a moment ago. Cheyenne knew he was gone.

"No. This isn't right. It isn't fair! He's changed. He was sorry! Didn't they know he was sorry? It should be okay now! This isn't fair! *GODDAMMIT!*"

She sobbed as she gathered him up.

The pain was almost more than she could bear. It might have broken her in that moment if not for one thing, the one thing that had become her greatest joy and her greatest source of strength—her husband.

As she cried, she held that poor abused boy to her chest.

Faulkner wrapped them up in his big strong arms and held them both to his.

EPILOGUE

FAULKNER STEPPED up to the podium to address the crowd. The press, the politicians, and most importantly, the community, had all turned out for today's grand opening of Riverside's new rec center for teens, Delgado's Grotto.

"I should probably start off by thanking you all for coming today. This center holds a special place in my wife's heart and mine. Six months ago, a young man, only seventeen years old, had been used and manipulated and twisted until he'd been turned into a living weapon. Then that weapon had been aimed directly at my wife and me. Not just us either, but law enforcement in general. I'm sure most of you have read the story of how he'd come to the city with explosives and a plan that had been drilled into him so relentlessly, he'd become brainwashed. And mass destruction was his mission."

Emotion threatened to undermine his composure so he took a breath and his eyes fell on Shy, sitting whole and beautiful with their daughter on her knee. He and Shy were closer now than ever before; their experience in the club in New York had been more than he'd dared hoped for. They'd enjoyed it so much they had even made a couple visits to some of the local clubs as their horizons broadened and the trust they shared deepened. Looking at her now, surrounded by his SEAL team and their families in the front row, made a feeling bloom in his chest that was larger than he even had words for. They centered him, his family, his heart and soul, so after a moment he was able to continue.

"His was a story that is unfortunately all too common. Not to the extreme that he was driven, but common nonetheless. If he'd had a place like this center available to him growing up, a place filled with people who cared, would he have been driven to the same conclusions? We'll never know now. But I like to think the answer to that is no. That he would have grown to be a man free of turmoil and would have found love and a family and would have lived a life he could have been proud of."

He paused for effect, hoping that the *what ifs* settled into the crowd's minds like a wakeup call.

"No child should be raised in anger and hate. With resources like this center, our hope is that Miguel's story will never be played out in another child's life. Miguel's story *does* have a silver lining that you would've heard if you've heard anything about him. Without any outside influence, and against all the odds, Miguel became a hero. He changed his course of action all on his own and gave his life to stop the destruction he'd been used to implement. His last words were those of a hero, his only concern was for the safety of others and reversing the deadly chain of events he'd set in play."

Looking over the people gathered, Faulkner saw tears on many of the solemn faces and hoped that they settled in deep enough to make a lasting impression, not one that would be easily forgotten when the monotony of daily life returned.

"With help from the Wellington/Marshall Foundation, Miguel's story will live on in this center. But I'm going to let them tell you about that in a minute. First, I just wanna say something about that day. I looked in Miguel's eyes that afternoon and I didn't see a terrorist or a killer. I saw a scared and confused kid who was trying to right his wrongs. A kid who will never know that his sacrifice would ignite a nation and bring change to so many communities, not just his own. A kid who proved to us all, it's never too late to do the right thing."

He stepped back and motioned for Trevor to come forward and take over.

Trevor would fill them in on the state of the art arcade and the go-cart track, as well as all the other wonderland-like features the center had in store. He'd get the bigwigs in the audience stirred up and reaching deep into their pockets, which was a good thing since the center would run on donations.

Thanks to Miguel's story, the center had already received more money than they'd even hoped for. Enough to fully fund the center and its staff for the next three years, but Trevor Wellington didn't let that put a damper on his speech. He spoke with the enthusiasm of a Baptist preacher on Sunday, and today was no different. People were cheering and crying by turns as his strong voice rang with conviction. He had them eating out of the palm of his hand.

Faulkner looked to his wife again. The loss of the kid had hit them both hard, but it was even more so for her. It helped knowing that Miguel's useless excuse of a mother was locked away.

Miguel had left behind a laptop in the grimy motel he'd stayed in while in New York. On it were two video files of confessions. The first, labeled

Vengeance is Mine, had been incomplete. Miguel's face had been covered in a ski mask and it was obviously a recording he'd intended to release after the bombing. He'd spewed propaganda about police brutality and the oppression of the poor, but already his conviction had waned. His voice had shaken and he'd stopped and restarted dozens of times. One failed attempt after another as he'd tried to spout the rhetoric that'd been drilled into him.

The second file had been titled *If I die.* There they'd seen the true Miguel. His face had been ravaged by tears as he'd looked into the camera and confessed. He'd told of his brothers and his childhood and weaved a story of abuse and torment that was hard to watch.

After he'd outlined the task that he'd been given and his harrowing journey to accomplish it, he'd confessed how he couldn't go through with it. He'd known he was going to die and he'd believed it was the only way. He'd asked for forgiveness and signed off. The time stamp on that video was less than a half hour from when Shy and the others had stumbled upon him.

They hadn't been able to save Miguel, but every day both Dude and Shy helped save others. It didn't make his loss any easier, but *this* did, he thought as he looked at the building behind them. This sure as hell did. The boy's death, though senseless, had brought *this* about—not just here but in cities across the nation, and by God, that was something. He hoped the kid knew somehow. He liked to think he did.

When Trevor finished with a rousing flurry of words that got the crowd to their feet, Faulkner made his way off the platform and to his family.

As he wrapped them in his arms, Faulkner thought again of what might have been if Miguel hadn't found bravery within himself. The bombs he'd rigged and where he'd placed them couldn't have toppled the entire building, but the destruction would have been massive and lives would have been lost for sure. Maybe even theirs.

So he held his family a little tighter, a little longer, and sent one more prayer of thanks to the heavens. He took it as a sign when Shy lifted her beautiful face and just as his lips met hers, the clouds parted. They were bathed in the warmth of a brilliant ray of sunshine while they shared a tender kiss and their daughter cooed happily between them.

Also by Lainey Reese

New York Series

A Table for Three
Damaged Goods
Innocence Defied
Embracing the Fall
Protecting New York

Stand Alone

Guarding Nadia

ABOUT THE AUTHOR

Lainey lives in beautiful Washington State. She's the youngest of five and has always wanted to be a writer. Her first novel, -A Table for Three- was nominated for best debut novel of 2010 by the Romance Review and marked a dream come true for Lainey.

With her third published release -Damaged Goods-, Lainey saw another of her dreams realized when she took a leap of faith to become a full-time author and left the safety net of a day job behind. Now she spends her days writing, with her dog at her feet and a cat curled in her lap, and asks herself a dozen times a day; how'd I ever get so lucky?

lainey@laineyreese.com
www.laineyreese.com

facebook.com/lainey.reese.7
bookbub.com/authors/lainey-reese

More Books in the Special Forces: Operation Alpha World!

Brynne Asher: Blackburn
Denise Agnew: Dangerous to Hold
Shauna Allen: Awakening Aubrey
Shauna Allen: Defending Danielle
Shauna Allen: Rescuing Rebekah
Shauna Allen: Saving Scarlett
Shauna Allen: Saving Grace
Jennifer Becker: Hiding Catherine
Julia Bright: Saving Lorelei
Victoria Bright: Surviving Savage
Victoria Bright: Going Ghost
Victoria Bright: Jostling Joker
Kendra Mei Chailyn: Beast
Kendra Mei Chailyn: Barbie
Kendra Mei Chailyn : Pitbull
Melissa Kay Clarke: Rescuing Annabeth
Melissa Kay Clarke: Safeguarding Miley
Samantha A. Cole: Handling Haven
Samantha A. Cole: Cheating the Devil
Sue Coletta: Hacked
KaLyn Cooper: Rescuing Melina
Liz Crowe: Marking Mariah
Jordan Dane: Redemption for Avery

Jordan Dane: Fiona's Salvation

Riley Edwards: Protecting Olivia

Riley Edwards: Redeeming Violet

Nicole Flockton: Protecting Maria

Nicole Flockton: Guarding Erin

Nicole Flockton: Guarding Suzie

Nicole Flockton: Guarding Brielle

Casey Hagen: Shielding Nebraska

Casey Hagen: Shielding Harlow

Casey Hagen: Shielding Josie

Desiree Holt: Protecting Maddie

Kathy Ivan: Saving Sarah

Kathy Ivan: Saving Savannah

Kathy Ivan: Saving Stephanie

Jesse Jacobson: Protecting Honor

Jesse Jacobson: Fighting for Honor

Jesse Jacobson: Defending Honor

Jesse Jacobson: Summer Breeze

Silver James: Rescue Moon

Silver James: SEAL Moon

Silver James: Assassin's Moon

Becca Jameson: Saving Sofia

Kate Kinsley: Protecting Ava

Heather Long: Securing Arizona

Heather Long: Guarding Gertrude

Heather Long: Protecting Pilar

Heather Long: Covering Coco

Kirsten Lynn: Joining Forces for Jesse
Margaret Madigan: Bang for the Buck
Margaret Madigan: Buck the System
Margaret Madigan: Jungle Buck
Margaret Madigan: December Chill
Rachel McNeely: The SEAL's Surprise Baby
Rachel McNeely: The SEAL's Surprise Bride
KD Michaels: Saving Laura
KD Michaels: Protecting Shane
Wren Michaels: The Fox & The Hound
Wren Michaels: The Fox & The Hound 2
Wren Michaels: Shadow of Doubt
Wren Michaels: Shift of Fate
Wren Michaels: Steeling His Heart
Kat Mizera: Protecting Bobbi
Mary B Moore: Force Protection
LeTeisha Newton: Protecting Butterfly
LeTeisha Newton: Protecting Goddess
LeTeisha Newton: Protecting Vixen
LeTeisha Newton: Protecting Heartbeat
MJ Nightingale: Protecting Beauty
MJ Nightingale: Betting on Benny
MJ Nightingale: Protecting Secrets
Sarah O'Rourke: Saving Liberty
Debra Parmley: Protecting Pippa
Lainey Reese: Protecting New York
Jenika Snow: Protecting Lily

As you know, this book included at least one character from Susan Stoker's books. To check out more, see below.

Delta Force Heroes Series

Rescuing Rayne (FREE!)
Rescuing Aimee (novella)
Rescuing Emily
Rescuing Harley
Marrying Emily
Rescuing Kassie
Rescuing Bryn
Rescuing Casey
Rescuing Sadie
Rescuing Wendy
Rescuing Mary (Oct 2018)
Rescuing Macie (April 2019)

Badge of Honor: Texas Heroes Series

Justice for Mackenzie (FREE!)
Justice for Mickie
Justice for Corrie
Justice for Laine (novella)
Shelter for Elizabeth
Justice for Boone
Shelter for Adeline

Shelter for Sophie
Justice for Erin
Justice for Milena
Shelter for Blythe
Justice for Hope (Sept 2018)
Shelter for Quinn (Feb 2019)
Shelter for Koren (June 2019)
Shelter for Penelope (Oct 2019)

SEAL of Protection Series

Protecting Caroline (FREE!)
Protecting Alabama
Protecting Fiona
Marrying Caroline (novella)
Protecting Summer
Protecting Cheyenne
Protecting Jessyka
Protecting Julie (novella)
Protecting Melody
Protecting the Future
Protecting Kiera (novella)
Protecting Dakota

SEAL of Protection: Legacy Series

Securing Caite (Jan 2019)
Securing Sidney (May 2019)
Securing Piper (Sept 2019)

Securing Zoey (TBA)
Securing Avery (TBA)
Securing Kalee (TBA)

New York Times, USA Today and *Wall Street Journal* Bestselling Author Susan Stoker has a heart as big as the state of Texas where she lives, but this all American girl has also spent the last fourteen years living in Missouri, California, Colorado, and Indiana. She's married to a retired Army man who now gets to follow *her* around the country.
She debuted her first series in 2014 and quickly followed that up with the SEAL of Protection Series, which solidified her love of writing and creating stories readers can get lost in.
If you enjoyed this book, or any book, please consider leaving a review. It's appreciated by authors more than you'll know.
www.stokeraces.com
www.AcesPress.com
susan@stokeraces.com